One moonlit night

One moonlit night

CARADOG PRICHARD

Translated from the Welsh by Philip Mitchell

A NEW DIRECTIONS CLASSIC

T O M A T I A N D M A R I

FOR THEIR ENDLESS PATIENCE AND TOLERANCE

Manufactured in the United States of America
New Directions books are printed on acid-free paper.
Published simultaneously in Canada by Penguin Books Canada Limited.
This translation first published in Great Britain in 1995 by Canongate Books. First published in 1997 as a New Directions Classic.

Library of Congress Cataloging-in-Publication Data
Prichard, Caradog, 1904-1980
  [Un Nos ola leuad.   English]
  One moonlit night / Caradog Prichard; translated by Philip Mitchell.
          p. cm. — (New Directions classics)
  ISBN 0-8112-1342-0
  1. World War, 1914-1918—Wales—Fiction.
  2. Boys—Wales—Fiction. 3. Wales—Fiction.
  I. Mitchell, Philip.   II. Title.   III. Series.
  PB2298.P7N6713 1997
  891.6'6328—DC21   96-51842
                                                CIP

New Directions Books are published for James Laughlin
by New Directions Publishing Corporation,
80 Eighth Avenue, New York 10011

SECOND PRINTING

TRANSLATOR'S NOTE

In translating *Un Nos Ola Leuad* into English, I have relied
heavily upon two principles: *faithfulness* in that I have tried to
keep as close as possible to the meaning of the original text, while
also tuning in to the sounds of the words, their relationships to
each other and the hints and allusions which each word carries
with it, and *function* in that I have striven to produce a narrative
which will evoke in the English language reader the same strong
feelings that the original work evokes in the Welsh reader.

The following paragraphs may be of help to readers unfamiliar
with the history of Wales, its language and its culture.

The expletive, 'Dew!' In Welsh, as in English, expletives tend
to be rooted in religion. The difference is that, in Welsh society,
religious expletives are regarded as significantly more shocking
than are the corresponding expressions in England. The mild
expletive 'Dew!' occurs throughout the narrative of *Un Nos Ola
Leuad* and has been retained in the translation. The word has
no intrinsic meaning but is used throughout Wales as a means
of approaching, yet ultimately avoiding, the very much stronger
exclamation 'Duw!' (God).

Placenames. Most of the novel's placenames are reproduced
in their original Welsh form. However, those names rich in
symbolism or which carry essential meaning have been rendered
in English. A glossary of these names can be found at the end of
the book.

Personal names. The use of hereditary or family surnames is
a relatively recent phenomenon in Wales. The first surnames
appeared about 1600 but, even then, the practice spread both

slowly and cautiously. The result is that, today, just a handful of names dominates all others. However, the problems of identification inherent in the situation are overcome, at a local level, by the ingenious application of nicknames which are used in addition to, or instead of, the original surname—in *One Moonlit Night*, we meet characters such as Bob Milk Cart (a milkman), Owen the Coal (a fuel merchant), Johnny Beer Barrel (his father runs the pub), Price the School (a teacher), Little Bob School (Price's son), Will Ellis Porter (a baggage carrier), Johnny Edwards Butcher (in the meat trade) and many, many more including one of the best known characters in Welsh literature—and probably the most lengthily-named—Emyr, Little Owen the Coal's Big Brother.

Other names. 'Settling-up Saturday' (referred to on page 57) is the nickname given to the first Saturday of each month following the *tâl mawr* (big payout) in the mines and quarries the previous Friday night.'

I would like to thank Glenys Roberts for her help, advice, support and encouragement without which this translation would not have been possible. *Diolch o galon*, Glenys.

Philip Mitchell

INTRODUCTION

One Moonlit Night was first published in the original Welsh in 1961. Caradog Prichard started it in 1955, intending to write it as 'a radio play for voices' like Dylan Thomas's *Under Milk Wood*. Both these writers were exiles in London, both stage-Welshmen somewhat the worse for drink. Caradog wanted to recollect, in some sort of tranquillity, the shattering upheavals of his youth, for this was to be a largely autobiographical novel – a cathartic work about a young boy being driven out of his mind by his family and social circumstances, reliving them 'one moonlit night' when he has returned to his home patch.

Caradog Prichard was born in 1904 in the town of Bethesda in the slate-quarrying area of north-west Wales. He died in London in 1980. His father had died when he was five months old, and there was a suspicion that he had been a 'traitor', a scab, during the Quarrymen's Strike of 1900–03. His mother gradually deteriorated and when he was in his late teens, he had to take her to the Mental Hospital in Denbigh, where she had been committed, and where she was to spend the rest of her life. His life and work were forever afterwards a confabulation. Many is the time I spoke to him and, after his death, his wife, and found it impossible without other sources to separate fact from fiction.

He had left Bethesda when he was seventeen to train as a journalist in Caernarfon, then in its heyday as the centre of Welsh-language newspaper and magazine publishing. He became part of a circle of young journalists and writers: daring and debonair young men, challenging the traditional Nonconformist taboos against drink, sex and prodigality. Caradog started writing poetry in this period, winning his first Eisteddfodic Crown in 1927, as well as writing his first journalistic pieces in English for Fleet Street, for the *Manchester Guardian*. But he was already enmeshed with that hospital in Denbigh where, as he later acknowledged, the other end of his uncut umbilical cord bound him to his mad mother. However far he went from her, that cord still held fast.

In 1928 he moved to the *Western Mail* in Cardiff, where he also did a degree in Welsh as a mature student, married a local girl, and won two more Crowns. Then on to London in 1936, to the *News Chronicle*. But emotionally he remained fixated in Bethesda and in his late adolescence. Whether in Caernarfon, Cardiff, London or India, he was always an exile, internally and externally, and as a writer his work is almost all to do with his childhood and the trauma he suffered then. His relationships with Bethesda and with his mother were pathological, but he managed to make enduring literature out of them. He wrote four prize-winning odes and this uniquely fine novel, *Un Nos Ola Leuad* (*One Moonlit Night*), as well as a few pot-boilers.

As a poet, he broke all records at the National Eisteddfod by winning the Crown three years in succession. They changed the rules afterwards, to prevent such an occurence happening again. Each of the prize-winning poems was about his mother's undying grief. Many years later, in 1962, when she had died, he won the Chair at the Eisteddfod with a poem in which he wrote as if he were a priest crying in the wilderness. And it was at this time too that he wrote *One Moonlit Night* as well. The first of the Crown poems, 'Y Briodas' (The Marriage), opens thus (the following rough translations are mine):

> Oh cold, tear-less Sadness. Could I but
>   have the relief of crying
> Like comforting summer sun to thaw my woe;
> I'll go again upon my knees for the solace of the Hands
> He proffers when the time comes to carry the cross.

Between that 'tear-less sadness' and the incredible weeping

described in the penultimate chapter of *One Moonlit Night* lies the whole span Caradog Prichard's life and work. He was a tortured soul, who never shed his grief at his mother's madness yet still sought the solace of the one who bore the Cross. Caradog's mother never managed to thaw her grief into tears. When he took his first Crown to show her in the Mental Hospital in Denbigh, she plonked it on her head and sang a hymn:

> I would wish to be forever
> A gem in Jesus's crown.
> Sounding forth his praises
> Lauding him in song

What a harrowing experience that must have been: seeing his mad mother, still using the language of religion but unable to shed her guilt-ridden grief for her husband, a grief which had shattered her spirit and mind. How awful it must have been to feel responsible for such a creature, and to have to do so for most of his life, since she lived to the age of seventy-nine. Wherever he was, he remained loyal to her, perhaps I should say tied to her. Most of the time he went as far away from her as he could although, according to his autobiography, he once returned to his work in Caernarfon to find that she had locked herself in the coalhouse because the authorities were trying to evict her from her home – and his – because she couldn't pay the rent. He asserted later that he was still waiting for someone to wake him up and say the incident was a nightmare. It could be said that he was always waiting for someone to wake him up and tell him that most of his life was a nightmare.

In his remarkable book on Kafka, the Italian critic, Pietro Citati, discusses the anguish of this Czech writer. He shows how this painfully introspective man gives us a glimpse of that hell which is within all of us. Citati reminds us of that scarifying, hysterical tension which made Kafka write of feeling that 'his frontal bone blocks his path; he beats his forehead against his own forehead until he makes it bleed'.

Caradog's inner world wasn't quite so dark. He retained a

faith in God, who wasn't the censorious, unforgiving God of the Czech's world, and he also retained some sense of humour and hope. Caradog could write:

> Between me and the land of the great secret
>   There is a long, dark hall,
> Where is heard the tinkling of ice bells
> Through cold winter nights and long summer days,
> But beyond its perplexing night there is a dawn
> Of the country of the Clear Light.

But the two authors have much in common in their sense of inescapable, mad-making anguish.

Caradog Prichard did, indeed, stay with his mother in mind and heart all his life. He wrote about her, spoke for her – especially in his poetry – and visited her when he was within reach, but he also resented this dependency, hated her at times. He went so far as to prohibit flowers at her funeral. No wonder he idolised and idealised mother figures in myths and, in *One Moonlit Night*, represented the mountain as forever pregnant. As he said himself, about the period at the beginning of the Second World War:

> the connection with the Mental Hospital – the asylum – in Denbigh remained a perpetual sore. There amongst the residents was the mother who inspired all my previous [Crown] poems and the umbilical cord not yet cut.

Time and time again we are reminded by him that that relationship with his mother comes between him and females in matters sexual.

> Looking back, I believe that it was at this time [when his mother had begun to break down] I felt the crack in my personality. Up to then I had been bold and confident, a fierce fighter and renowned as a bit of a bully amongst the local lads. But after the shock of realising my mother was beginning to lose her mind there was a marked deterioration in my character. I would walk stealthily along the streets of the village as if afraid of my shadow.

He tried to form relationships with girls but always thought of his mother; even when he saw a gorgeous girl in far-away India, his mind raced back to that ward in the Mental Hospital in Denbigh. He kept on writing about mental illness all his life and often walked a Kierkegaardian tight-rope between faith and despair, life and perdition, heaven and hell, in his life as well as in his work. Not that Caradog Prichard was a morose, morbid individual: he was gregarious and fun-loving, fond of cigars and his drink to a fault. He could seem to be a happy-go-lucky creature by his antics, his buffoonery, his hiring of white Rolls Royces on special occasions, and all his flourishes. But he remained a tortured soul. No amount of travel, drink, acting out, cathartic writing, even transcultural migration to Fleet Street and the pubs on the Strand, not even offering up his woe to the Crucified, Risen and Ascended Christ, none of all that enabled him to resolve his anguish. On at least one occasion he tried to end it all but remembered nothing of the experience:

> The next thing I remember is sitting in a chair facing the station-master of one of the stations between the Strand and Golders Green. I can see his face this minute, sitting across his desk from me. He had a little yellow moustache and he wore gold-rimmed spectacles. He looked at me with a serious and pitying gaze.
>
> 'You're one of the luckiest men under the sun,' he said. 'You were lying across the track within an inch or two of the electric rails. And if we'd been a minute or two later getting you from there you wouldn't be here listening to me.'
>
> There is no doubt in my mind but that this was a deliberate attempt, under the command of the subconscious, to take leave of this existence voluntarily. For this was the exact period when I had been tossing and turning in my mind the idea of a poem about self-destruction.

Within a month of that Eisteddfod in Denbigh, war had broken out. Caradog enlisted and was eventually sent to India to serve in Intelligence in Cimla. His wife Mati was left to visit the mother in Denbigh as often as she could. He came back after the war, to the *Daily Telegraph*, and was overjoyed when his only child, Mari, was born in 1947.

He toyed with the idea of returning to Wales, but always vacillated and eventually only came back for a year, on an Arts Council Bursary. But by then he was too old and disillusioned to make anything worthwhile of the experience. In 1954, however, his mother died, at last, and was buried with her husband and their son, William, who died when five weeks old. There had been two other children, boys who were older than Caradog, but they left home and went off as far as they could once they were old enough. It had been Caradog who had carried the cross. He felt he could now at least try to look again at those early, searing traumas he had experienced.

The two great events which formed the background to the novel, as Prichard himself said, were the great, though unsuccessful strike by the quarreymen in the Bethesda area in 1900–03, and the quasi-religious revivals of 1904–05 in Wales. There was, too, the Great War as a backdrop where thousands of young Welshmen were being decimated in far and foreign fields. It was a war for which those men were entirely unprepared by their religious upbringing, which was almost devoid of any theological or philosophical content. The spiritual life of the nation was at a low ebb, drained by the emotionalism of the revivals, which can now, alas, be seen as a phenomenon in the history of Welsh Nonconformity.

As with Wales, so with the individuals and community Caradog presents to us. The novel shows a whole community falling apart along old cleavage lines; a way of life warping, distorting, shattering and splintering, losing touch with the outside world and with its own past. This is quite a different picture from the one usually given in Welsh literature about this period and place, where the Welsh are personified like the peasantry in nineteenth-century Russian novels, as epic heroes in a struggle against the alienated aristocracy. In the Welsh case, the aristocracy was composed of the Anglicised or Anglican slate-, land-, or coal-owners. Caradog, though, also saw the fault lines within the people themselves: the decay of spirituality, the hypocrisy and sin. He makes explicit what is only implicit in the novels of Daniel Owen, the late nineteenth-century writer and the father of the Welsh novel. Owen subtly satirised the hypocrisy of the Nonconformist world he belonged to. Caradog lived in that world, but as an Anglican was an outsider on the inside. Both authors however straddled the two traditions of Welsh prose: the social chronicle and the story of the individual soul. Both also eschewed the sentimentalism which had masked reality in so much nineteenth-century Welsh literature. Of course, many of these faults and failings were common to most rural or remote areas in the last century, not just Victorian Britain and Ireland. These repressions and inhibitions had to lead to some sort of explosion or breakdown as they had, in general, little moral or religious bases, or those had been forgotten. No wonder that 'mere anarchy was loosed upon the world' of Wales by the Great War.

Caradog, like James Joyce, had a genius for making words resonate in all our senses as well as exciting the intellect. This novel is replete with religious and philosophical ideas and concepts. At the same time it reminds us of the whole gamut of human emotions, makes us smell and taste things, feel the texture of a hand or a cheek, hear forgotten sounds, see visions as well as vistas; and two other senses, the erotic and the spiritual, are not neglected.

Like Joyce, again, he is also master at varying his style: from somewhat formal narrative to colourful dialect; from the language of children to that of the old; from the realistic to the artificial; from Chagalian magic to the relentlessly objective; from the cerebral to the lyrical; the innocent to the fiendish; the plaintive to the joyous; from the language of small, racy gossip to that of the Psalms.

When all is said and done, *One Moonlit Night* is about a fraught, frightening relationship between a little boy and his distraught, grieving mother: a terrifyingly sensitive, sensuous and imaginative child, his mind like raw flesh, hurt to the quick by so many events which had almost driven him mad.

He became over-protective towards his mother, blamed his father for abandoning her, and tended to shun male models of behaviour. What had the father done to the mother to leave her so bereft, anguished and poor, and blindly faithful to him: a courageous, difficult mother, 'always crying away quietly about something or other'? It was only in bed he could get close to her and be comforted. No wonder he pined, longed – as 'the doe longs for the running stream' – yearned to be cuddled and embraced. He gets a semblance of comfort from Grace next door, from the touch of eighteen-year-old Ceri's bosom, and from his contemplation of the Mother Queen in the mountain, eternally at her appointed time, with her bounteous, maternal and loving body. He has no model of fatherhood, nor the relationship between a mother and father, and his only experience of adult sexual behaviour is seeing the schoolmaster taking simple little Jini behind the school to sin secretly and slyly against her.

The spiritual is palpably present for him, and for his mother, in the existence of angels, Heaven and Hell, Christ's Passion, and the Resurrection and Ascension. But these have not been integrated with the other, experiential realities which lurk under the skin: the Black Lake which holds such a fatal attraction, those dangerous feelings of lust as he comes to puberty, his need for bodily comfort, and the wrath towards the fate that had made his mother bereft and himself a poor and virtually orphaned child.

Frank O'Connor has a story called 'My Oedipus Complex', where a young lad feels angry towards his father who has returned from the Great War, a stranger, and 'usurped' the son's place in his mother's bed. It is possible to feel that sort of ire against an absent father as well, for having left the son in that maternal bed.

There, I have mentioned the Oedipus complex, which is not such a rare phenomenon in Welsh literature. I'm not alluding to specific acts, to anything vile, but the inevitable problems associated with growing up and leaving one's mother's side, in the case of a son, and cleaving, as the scriptures say, to another female. It is something which can lead to a sort of perversion in some, especially when there is already a store of negative feelings within the young person. If he has a live conscience and is a sensitive soul, then pathological guilt can consume him, break him, as he is torn between loyalty, body and soul, to the mother on the one hand and his driving instinct to form a bodily relationship with a female of his own age. This conflict leads to prostitution in Joyce's *Portrait of the Artist as a Young Man*, and in a few it can lead to violent sexual crimes.

This stricken boy, guilt-ridden at his perceived failure to care for his mother, is 'tempted' by the natural attraction and innocent sexual vivacity of little Jini, with her blue eyes and nubile body. He returns 'one moonlit night' bent now on doing his real penance, not to Jini or even to God, but to his mother, and to the Queen of the Black Lake. We relive the events of his childhood on the way to the lake and are reminded subtly about Christ's Atonement, and prepared for an act of self-immolation. The end is accomplished to the accompaniment of a De Profundis-like psalm, an invocation of all the mother-figures in his life.

What is great and memorable about this classic work of childhood is the remarkable sense of style and the rare combination of the criminal and the spiritual, of the individual and the communal, worthy of a Dostoyevsky. It is a great, panoramic novel, encompassing so much of the human condition everywhere and in all ages, and redeeming by art much that seems irretrievably vile in that experience. Philip Mitchell's fine translation of this work gives to English readers, for the first time, an opportunity to share to the full the qualities of this Welsh masterpiece.

Harri Pritchard Jones

I

I'LL GO AND ASK Huw's Mam if he can come out to play. Can Huw come out to play, O Queen of the Black Lake? No, he can't, he's in bed and that's where you should be, you little monkey, instead of going round causing a riot at this time of night. Where were you two yesterday making mischief and driving village folk out of their minds?

What village folk out of their minds? It's not us that's driving them out of their minds, it's them that are going out of their minds themselves. We weren't anywhere yesterday except walking about. I got Go on there! and Whoa there! first thing in the morning, fetching the Tal Cafn cattle from Pen y Foel and picking a capful of mushrooms on Ffridd Wen after pulling up a few of Owen Gorlan's potatoes for Mam on the way home.

This is why Huw and me went to the back door of Margaret Lewis's shop for a pennorth of apples, cos I hadn't had any breakfast before I went to school cos Mam had gone to do the washing at the Vicarage. We were just finishing eating them as we got to School and the clock was striking nine. And I know who threw the clump of turf through the window while we were saying prayers, and hit Price the School on the side of the head while he was kneeling down. It was Owen, Mary Plums's boy, and Little Dai from the Black Shop. They only left Standard Four at the beginning of the year. I saw them both legging it through the Graveyard just like two evil spirits among the gravestones.

And we hadn't done anything when Price the School caned us. He was in a terrible temper all morning. But when he came

1

back from The Blue Bell after playtime with his face as red as a beetroot, he went berserk and started thrashing everybody. Huw and me just happened to get in the way of his cane. But after he went to Standard Four to fetch Little Jini Pen Cae and took her off with him through the far door, we didn't see anything of him till the bell went for dinner time.

It was Huw wanting to go to the Quarry to tell Jini's dad, that's why we went along Post Lane. There was no school at our school in the afternoon because it was Ascension Day but there was school in the Chapel schools. We would have gone to the Quarry too except that there were a lot of people standing by Stallions Gate in front of Catrin Jane's house in Lower Lane, and Little Will Policeman's Dad was standing by the door watching two men carrying the furniture out and putting it in a pile in the middle of the lane and Catrin Jane had locked herself in the coal shed and was screaming and shouting: Go away you devils, you've no right to go into my house. Dew, it was a fine afternoon as well. Never mind the old Quarry, said Huw, we'll go for a picnic to the top of Rallt Ddu.

That's why we went to Ann Jones's shop, because we only had enough money to buy one bottle of pop and we wanted four, and two currant cakes because Nell Fair View and Kate White Houses were coming after us. You go and buy one bottle, said Huw, I'll get the others. He was a sly one, Huw. I'm sure Ann Jones had seen him but she was frightened of saying anything because she was afraid of you, O Queen of the Black Lake.

Before the two girls caught up to us, who should come up Stables Lane and meet us by the Pen Lôn Gate but Little Harry the Clogs with his basket on his arm and laughing hee! hee! hee! through his beard. Give us a quick look, Harry, said Huw, and Harry put his basket down, and then he opened his flies and pulled his willy out. Hee! hee! hee! he said through his beard and pulled it back in again quick as wink just like a jack-in-the-box. Hee! hee! hee! he said again then picked up his basket and off he went on his way. Hee! hee! hee! said the two girls behind us. Watch yourself, Nell Fair View, said Huw as we were going through the gate. And you as well,

Kate White Houses, I said. But they still came after us through the gate.

It was Huw who went first to hide behind the wall and then I did the same, and they only pretended to run across the field when we ran after them. It was Huw that caught Nell first and threw her onto the ground and lifted her skirt up. That's why I did the same thing with Kate, because Huw had the pop bottles. I was only carrying the two currant cakes. And there they both were, lying on their backs with their skirts up with us two staring down at them.

It was Huw that had the poacher's pocket, that's why he was carrying the bottles. But it was the two currant cakes I pulled out of my pocket that made Nell pull her skirt down and sit up and tell Kate to do the same. They knew full well we were going to have a picnic.

Dew! It was a fine afternoon. The sun was making the hay smell so good and the air was so clear I could see Mam putting clothes on the line at the bottom of Vicarage Field. That's why it's so fine, said Nell, because it's Ascension Day. But Kate got up and started crying. I'll tell my Mam, she said, crying like I don't know what, and ran off home. And Nell went after her when she'd drunk her bottle of pop and scoffed a big piece of currant cake.

Then Huw wanted to know why Churchpeople went to church on Ascension Day and I said to him: Don't you know, Huw? No, I don't, Huw said. Well, because Jesus Christ went up to Heaven like a balloon on Thursday after He rose from the dead, of course. All the good people are going to rise from the dead, everyone in the Graveyard, no matter how heavy their gravestones are, and go up like balloons just like Jesus Christ. But it's down to Hell we'll be going, you'll see, for stealing Ann Jones's pop bottles.

What are you doing Huw?

Making this pile of stumps into a cigarette so we can have a smoke. Moi can smoke coltsfoot leaves and he says he's seen Little Harry the Clogs collecting dried dung on Post Lane and smoking that. Do you think Griffith Evans Braich will be allowed to go to Heaven after splitting his head open when he got killed on Bonc Rhiwia in the quarry?

He's sure to be allowed to go, I said, cos the boys in the choir got tuppence each for going to the funeral.

He'll look horrible, said Huw. Try a little smoke.

Heurch! Heurch! Dew, I feel sick. Would you like to work in the Quarry, Huw?

Sure I would. I'm getting long trousers when I pass Standard Four, and Mam says I can go the minute I'm fourteen.

I don't want to go, Huw. Mam's said I can try for a scholarship and go to County School if I pass, and then go and see the world and make a lot of money.

He was a right one, that Arthur Tan Bryn, eh? Left County School to join the army, said Huw. He got to see the world, anyway, and Moi says he's killed a lot of Germans and they're going to put his name on the Memorial.

Dew, I want to throw up, I said. And we both ran across the field and buried our faces in the water in Ffrwd Rhiw until we were nearly choking.

If you open your eyes you can see the bottom, said Huw. Heurch! Heurch. That's how Will Pen Pennog drowned, but he drowned himself because he had cancer. They say smoking causes cancer and gives you lockjaw sometimes.

Dew, I'll never smoke again.

Wipe your mouth, said Huw, then we'll go to White Houses to fetch Moi so we can go to the Sheep Field to collect pignuts. They've fired the shot for hometime in the Quarry. Moi's Uncle Owen will have arrived home and they'll be having quarry supper. Maybe we'll get a piece of bread and butter from Moi's Mam to take the taste of that ruddy smoking away.

Who should come to meet us at Post Lane, just before we crossed Stables Bridge, with a huge trunk on his back, but Will Ellis Porter, with his nose nearly touching the ground and his two knees sticking out through the holes in his trousers as though they were trying to run on ahead of him.

Are you scared of him, Huw?

Yes, a little bit, sometimes.

4

Me too.

Never mind, he can't do anything to us with the trunk on his back. How goes it, Will Ellis?

Heurch! Heurch! You lazy little devils; been playing truant again. Heurch! Heurch!

Watch yourself Huw, he's going to have a fit.

Heurch! Heurch! And the trunk went clinkadyclonk off Will Ellis's back and he was rolling in the dust in the middle of the lane, with his tongue out and his eyes like two big gooseberries.

No, don't run, Huw said, he won't do anything to you. He can't stand up.

I went back very slowly when I saw Huw still beside him and I was close enough to him to see white froth coming out of his mouth, just like Ike Williams's horse when he was going up Allt Bryn with a load, and Little Owen the Coal was whipping him.

We'd better be off, before he comes to, said Huw.

I'd already reached the far end of White Houses before Huw had crossed Stables Bridge.

Ann Jones the Shop's brother has come back from America, we told Moi's Uncle Owen, so we'd have an excuse to go in. But he didn't lift his head up from his meat and potatoes. Moi just winked at us, telling us to stay.

Huw, said Moi's Mam, go to Ann Jones' shop for a pennorth of snuff and say it's me that's sending you, and say I'm glad to hear that Griffith Jones has come home safe from America.

But Moi's Uncle Owen kept his head down on his plate.

There'll be a hell of a row here in a minute, you'll see, Huw said quietly as he went out.

Have some bread and butter, chick, said Moi's Mam. And then Moi's Uncle Owen started growling like a dog and said something about paying for his food.

Shut your mouth and eat, said Moi's Mam. Dew, it was a great slice of bread she was cutting too, with thick butter on it. But I never got it. When the knife was halfway through the loaf, Uncle Owen jumped up and swept his plate and his meat and potatoes off the table and everything smashed to pieces and slithered all over the floor, and his eyes were flaming mad.

Come away, said Moi, who'd run round the table. Come on, out as fast as you can.

And as we were slinking through the door, what did we hear but the most terrible scream from Moi's Mam. I didn't look back till we were at Stables Bridge and Huw was coming back with the snuff.

Had we better go and fetch Little Will Policeman's Dad, Moi?

No, there's no need for that. He won't do anything to her. They're always like that.

We'd better go back and have a look, said Huw.

And the three of us were creeping back to the door, and what did we we see but Moi's Uncle Owen holding her hair with his left hand and pulling her head right back so you could see all her throat and Moi's Mam had her arm round him as though they were two lovers. She was holding the bread knife tight in her fist and he had the tuck knife from the dresser in his right hand, with the blade on the side of Moi's Mam's throat, like Johnny Edwards Butcher sticking that pig when we went to the slaughterhouse yesterday to ask for a bladder to play football with.

Here's your snuff, said Moi in the doorway. And Uncle Owen let go of her and sloped off to the back kitchen like a dog with his tail between his legs, without looking at anybody.

Thanks very much, chick, said Moi's Mam and started to fix her hair with a hairpin and took a pinch of snuff between her finger and thumb and put it into her nose and sneezed all over the place. Dew, Huw and me got some lovely bread and butter, then. And we were starving hungry, too.

Can Moi come out to play, we said, just to the Sheep Field to collect pignuts?

Don't you be late now, you little monkey, said Moi's Mam, you want to be up in the morning to go to the Quarry with Uncle Owen.

I won't, Mam. Come on lads, or it'll be getting dark.

Never mind, said Huw, there's a moon.

As we were coming up to the house at the end of White Houses, where Little Owen the Coal's Mam lives, who should be standing in the doorway with a great big hankie in her hand, wiping her nose, but Little Owen the Coal's Mam.

Come and see him, children, she said, sobbing. Come and see how pretty my little chick looks before they put the lid on him.

It's Emyr, Little Owen the Coal's Big Brother, said Moi quietly. It was today they brought him home from the asylum in Denbigh.

You don't say, said Huw, I didn't know.

And Little Owen the Coal's Mam was still saying: Come in and see my pretty little chick. Come on, said Moi.

And in we went after her. And she lit the lamp because the blinds were down and everywhere was dark. And there was Emyr, Little Owen the Coal's Big Brother, lying on the sofa in his coffin with a surplice like a choirboy's wrapped around him, and only his hands were in sight resting on his chest. Dew, he had long fingers. But his mouth made us want to laugh, except that Owen's Mam was sobbing and shouting: My pretty little chick.

We could see the roof of his mouth. And it was all crinkled as though he'd been thirsty for a long time.

Why didn't they close his mouth, I wonder? Huw said.

Maybe he was screaming after being beaten by those people at Denbigh, said Moi.

Or maybe he'd got lockjaw through smoking, I said.

When we came to Stallions Gate, who was in Lower Lane but a gang of the Quarry lads standing around Catrin Jane's furniture, and Little Will Policeman's Dad standing nearby and David Evans Snowdon View, who'd just been made a marker, saying something to them.

Hurry up, so we can hear what he's saying, said Moi.

When we'd hurried as slowly as we could into Lower Lane, pretending that we weren't listening, we heard the sound of a cat miaowing in the coal shed.

It's not a cat in there, said Huw, it's Catrin Jane still in there, crying.

We've got to do something lads, said David Evans Snowdon View to the others, with his hands in his trouser pockets scratching himself, and spitting heeerch-tuh after every word. We can't leave her in there all night, or God's judgement will be upon us just like it was on Ike Williams the Coal this afternoon, after he sent her out of her house. What? Didn't you hear about his horse dropping down dead in the stable after taking a load of coal to the top of Allt Bryn?

What about Old Margaret Williams' house? said one of the others. That's been empty ever since she was buried.

And David Evans gave a great heeerch-tuh and looked straight at Little Will Policeman's Dad and asked: Got anything to say to us, officer?

And he said: I can't see you and I can't hear you. So how can I have anything to say?

Let's get to it then, lads, said David Evans. Hey, you lazy little devils, come here and give us a hand.

And there we were for ages, carrying Catrin Jane's things and going backwards and forwards with them to Margaret Williams' empty old house, with Catrin Jane crying and miaowing in the coal shed the whole time.

Do you like walking down the street when all the shops have closed? Huw said after we'd finished.

No, not much.

Me neither.

Me neither, I said. Watch out Huw, Will Ellis Porter's over there sitting on the Post Office window sill. Let's walk on the other side.

No, it doesn't matter, said Huw, he doesn't remember anything about this afternoon, you know. He doesn't know what he's doing when he has a fit.

And Moi burst out laughing: Then he's not fit to have a fit, Ha! Ha! Jesus, what's the matter over there by the Chip Shop?

No, the house next to the chip shop, by The Blue Bell, said Huw. Hurry up lads, it's a fight!

And the the two of them ran on ahead of me and who was there when we got there but a lot of men and big boys who'd come out of the chip shop and The Blue Bell. And there was Owen Morris Llan, that one who went to be a sailor last year, and Bob Roberts Ceunant battering each other like I don't know what. Dew, I heard the sound of Bob Ceunant's fist like a Salvation Army Band drum hitting Owen Llan in the chest and him falling like a tree and lying on his stomach on the ground. Dew, I was shaking like a leaf and feeling like I was going to be sick when Little Will Policeman's Dad came down the street and everybody ran off.

Come on, lads, we'll never get any pignuts at this rate, said Moi.

Over the wall's the best way. David Jones the Keeper might be at the Wood Lane Gate.

So over the Lôn Newydd wall we went, and Huw's trousers got caught on some slate and ripped as he fell on his bum into the nettles.

Damn, said Huw, have you got a pin?

Don't make any noise in case Jones the Keeper catches us, said Moi.

So we went very quietly to where the pignuts were, trying not to tread on any twigs in case we made a noise. We could see okay, because it wasn't dark, because there was moonlight between the trees. But wow, I nearly had a fit once when this noise suddenly came from up above us; a sort of ruuurk-ruuurk-ruuurk like a threshing machine.

A pheasant, Moi said quietly.

But I'd already started wetting my trousers.

Without saying anything, Huw, who was ahead of us, suddenly stopped and turned to us with his finger over his lips, then dropped down to the ground on his stomach, and Moi and me did the same. The keeper, I said to myself and thought that we were about to get caught. But Huw and Moi went ahead very slowly and quietly on their stomachs, with me behind them doing the same, until Huw held his hand out behind him to tell us to stop.

And what did we see in front of us but Grace Ellen Shoe Shop and Frank Bee Hive lying down by a tree stump, and Frank had pulled her skirt up, just like we'd done with Kate and Nell in the afternoon, except that Frank was lying on top of her and nearly choking her, by the look of it.

Why was Frank lying on top of Grace Ellen and nearly choking her? I said to Huw when we'd finished collecting pignuts and gone over the Lôn Newydd wall into Post Lane.

I don't know.

Me neither.

They must have been playing, said Moi, the way people do when they get married.

But Grace Ellen and Frank Bee Hive aren't married, said Huw.

No, they shouldn't play like that, by rights, said Moi, but lots of people do. Uncle Owen does it with Mam sometimes, after they've been fighting. Jesus, what time is it, boys? I told Mam I'd be home soon.

It was half past nine by the clock on the Lockup, said Huw. Will you get a good hiding?

No. Not unless I don't get up to go to the Quarry with Uncle Owen tomorrow morning. Good night, lads.

Good night, Moi.

Good night, Moi.

Dew, the metal bit on the front of my shoe's loose, Huw. Ned Cwt Crydd can put a nail in it tomorrow morning. It makes a real noise in the street at night, eh Huw?

And I've torn my trousers, said Huw, I don't know what Mam'll say tomorrow morning.

Are you coming out to play, tomorrow, Huw?

I am, if Mam'll let me.

Alright, I've got ten coloured marbles I won off Moi yesterday. I'll bring them with me.

Alright. Good night, now.

Good night.

Dew, there's a nice smell from somewhere. Maybe it's coming from our house. It is, too. Hello Mam.

And she'd made a great roaring fire, and there she was sitting in the rocking chair. Fried potatoes and mushrooms.

Lor, I'm hungry, Mam.

Come on then, chick. You eat your fill. Where did you get those potatoes that were under the stairs?

I got them from Robin, the lad at Gorlan Farm. Dew, Mam, they're good fried like this with mushrooms.

You're sure you didn't steal them, aren't you, chick?

Steal them? No. Definitely not. I was coming back from fetching the cattle from Tal Cafn and who was pulling up potatoes in the Top Field but Robin. Here, take some he said when I said How goes it, Robin, take these home to your mother, and he put them in an old sack he had on the hedge. But don't tell anyone and tell your mother not to tell anyone. Okay, I said, thanks a lot, Robin.

Fair play to him, said Mam. How old is he now, d'you know?

He'd just left School in March when he went to work at Gorlan. Dew, these mushrooms are good. Are there any more, Mam?

No, you little guts, eat your bread and butter now.

Dew, I'll go and get another capful tomorrow morning. Did you have a hard day washing, Mam?

A bit tired, you know, love. Hurry up so you can go to bed and let me clear up and iron those clothes. The Vicarage wants them first thing in the morning. You can take them down for me if you will.

Course I will.

Where were you all afternoon after school? You haven't been up to mischief with that Huw today, have you?

No. What do you mean, up to mischief? We just went for a walk up to the top of Rallt Ddu because it was Ascension Day, and collected pignuts in the Sheep Field. Ann Jones the Shop's brother's come home from America.

You don't say. Did you see him?

No. Huw was saying. And they've put Catrin Jane from Lower Lane out of her house because she can't pay the rent to Ike Williams the Coal.

Who told you?

Nobody. Huw and Moi and me were going past and they asked us to help carry the furniture to Margaret Williams' old house. Ike Williams's horse dropped dead in the stable this afternoon. God's judgement upon him, David Evans Snowdon View said.

Yes, I'm sure it was. The nasty old so-and-so. Go to bed now, chick, you've got to be up first thing in the morning.

Alright, Mam. Good night.

But I couldn't sleep for the life of me, with the moon just like a big orange, shining on me through the skylight. So I got up and stood on the chair to open the window and stuck my head out. Dew, it was lovely and quiet, with just a slight sound in the air, like the sound of the River Sarnau, except that was a long way away, and the moon was zooming through the sky over Pen Foel Garnedd.

No, you silly fool, I said to myself, it's the clouds that are moving, not the moon. There wasn't a light in any of the windows anywhere. Just a tiny little light in White Houses. That's Moi's house, I'm sure. I hope old Moi didn't get a good hiding, anyway.

Yes, definitely, it was the clouds that were moving. That old moon's still shining through the skylight.

What's the matter, chick?

I can't sleep in this bedroom, Mam. I want to come and sleep in your bedroom with you.

Alright then, chick. Come and keep a warm place for me.

And when Mam came to bed, I went to sleep like a top, with my arms round her holding her tight.

And that's all that happened. We weren't anywhere except walking about and I didn't know until this morning, after I'd been to Ned Cwt Crydd to get a nail put in my shoe, that Moi's Uncle Owen had hanged himself in the toilet and that they'd taken Little Jini Pen Cae and Catrin Jane from Lower Lane to the Asylum. There's a full moon tonight. Why won't you let Huw come out to play, O Queen of the Black Lake?

2

ALRIGHT, I'LL go for a stroll up Post Lane as far as Stables Bridge to see if I can see Moi. And what did I see by The Blue Bell but a poster pasted on the wall to say there was a penny reading in Glanaber on Thursday night. It was just like that poster ages ago when Canon and Price the School came down Post Lane and Price the School said to Canon: Here's a clever little boy for you, and Canon gave me sixpence for not being able to read.

Is that so, said Canon, can he read English?

He can, by Jove, said the School, and I didn't know why he wanted to brag about it.

Alright, let me hear you read that, said Canon, and he tapped the poster on the wall with his stick. I was reading it okay until I came to Society. Socky-etty I said, and Canon roared with laughter.

No, said Price the School, really annoyed, So-sigh-ee-tee.

But Canon was still laughing his head off. Very good, my boy, honestly, he said, and reached into his trouser pocket and put a sixpenny piece in my hand.

No-one would ever think that Canon was such a kind man by looking at his face, cos he'd had smallpox a long time ago and that had left a scar on the side of his mouth that made him look as though he was smelling something nasty wherever he went. But when he was laughing his head off at something, like he was at me that time, there was no sign of the scar.

It was in the church pulpit that it showed best, especially when he was laying the law down or shouting Strive ye for salvation through Godinjesuschrist. It always made me think, when he was

13

shouting like that, about the story of the Day of Pentecost that Bob Milk Cart told us in Sunday School, and about the tongues of fire that came down from somewhere onto the heads of the Disciples and turned them into Apostles. Looking at Canon shouting in the pulpit, I used to think that a tongue of fire had come down through the church roof and stuck to his mouth. It was Mam who told me it was a smallpox scar.

Dew, Mam thought the world of him as well. You should have seen her ironing his surplice and his stole on the table at home. She always left his surplice till last and did all the men's and boys' first. Then she'd clear the table and place his surplice on it very slowly and run her fingers along every pleat in it. And it was bigger than any of the others too cos Canon was over six feet tall. He was the biggest Parson I ever saw.

Don't ask silly questions, Mam said when I asked her where he'd caught smallpox.

But why is there a scar by his mouth? I said.

Get out of my sight you little nuisance, said Mam. And I couldn't understand why she was so cross.

I was only asking, I said, watching the iron in her hand going backwards and forwards over the surplice, with her left hand holding the corner in case the iron went askew over the pleat.

I was thinking about Griffith Evans Braich, Mam. Do you remember washing his surplice on the Tuesday before he was killed in the Quarry and he didn't get to wear it the Sunday after? I was just thinking, I wonder if there'll be a scar on Griffith Evans' head in Heaven? And then I wondered if there'll be a scar on Canon's mouth when he's gone to Heaven.

And then Mam suddenly stopped ironing and started to cry.

What's up, Mam? Don't cry, I said, but I wasn't really worried because Mam was always crying quietly about something and I was used to it. But she was looking at me so strangely that I was sorry that I'd said anything to her.

No, there won't be, chick, she said with tears rolling down her cheeks and her laughing at the same time. There won't be a single scar on Griffith Evans Braich's head in Heaven and there won't be one on Canon's face either after he's gone there. And she stopped crying and went on with her ironing, singing.

I remember the words she was singing too: See beyond the mi-ists of time, O my s-o-oul behold the view, O my s-o-oul beho-o-old the view.

Dew, Mam had a good voice.

There's a light in the Vicarage study, too. Yes, I'm sure that's the study window, where the little light is between those two trees. But it's Azariah Jenkins who's sitting in the chair in front of that fire now, I'm sure. Him and his wife, perhaps. It was him who came here after Hughes the Parson, who came here after Canon. He was a nice chap, old Hughes, too. But he had TB and he wasn't a patch on Canon. He never gave me sixpence for not being able to read, anyway.

Dew, I used to like going to the Vicarage after school to help Mam with the washing all those years ago. Nell, Little Will Policeman's sister, and Gwen from Allt Bryn were the two maids there at that time. And even though Mam was much older than they were, they were great friends with her and still came to our house to see her after they got married. And it was a policeman that Nell married. Jones the New Policeman was her husband and I was never frightened of Jones the New Policeman cos Mam was such good friends with Nell, his wife. Gwen Allt Bryn was Frank Bee Hive's wife after she left the Vicarage.

Sit down there, love, said Nell when I went to the Vicarage for the first time after School to fetch Mam. I'll cut you a piece of bread and butter in two minutes. Dew, the Vicarage kitchen was a big kitchen. It was twice as big as our kitchen and front room put together. And what a lovely smell! Dew, I used to love the smell, with me being starving hungry. And then I sat in the chair wolfing my bread and butter. And who came through the passage door but Gwen Allt Bryn with a big silver tray in her hand cos she'd just taken tea to Canon and the visitors who were there.

Come to help your Mam? said Gwen. He's a good boy, isn't he Nell? You'll go to Heaven you know, lad, for helping your Mam.

Dew, Gwen had a pretty face. She had a prettier face than Nell, but Nell was the kinder of the two. She was always the first to give me a piece of bread and butter, every time I went there from school to help Mam with the clothes.

Is it Price the School that's there for tea? said Nell.

Yes, said Gwen putting the tray on the table. Have you had a hiding from Price yet? said Gwen.

No, course not, I said, lying.

Dew, you must be a right little angel then, said Gwen.

I watched Nell filling a big paper bag with lots of crusts and spare bread and butter and leftover bones from the Vicarage dinner, with lots of meat still on them, until the bag was full to bursting. And Mam came in with her hair a bit ruffled and her arms full of washing from the line in the Vicarage Field, ready to take them home to iron after they'd been folded and wrapped in one of the woollen sheets. Then the three of them sat down and had a cup of tea and talked about lots of people and I was still sitting on the chair and counting the big, red, square tiles on the kitchen floor and thinking Dew, this is a good place to play London with Huw and Moi, except we'd dirty the floor.

You carry the paper bag, said Mam, I can carry these, meaning the washing, and remember to hold it underneath in case it tears.

That was what I wanted her to say, of course, so I'd be able to put my hand into the paper bag on the way home when Mam wasn't looking. But I never used to touch anything until after we'd gone down the lane to the Vicarage gate and out into Post Lane here in case Canon saw me through the study window. Dew, I'm sure he would have been cross with me too if he'd seen me, but he never once saw me doing anything. Dew, the bread from the paper bag tasted good on the way home. Sometimes I'd find a piece of meat without any bone. Mam never used to speak on the way home, she was too tired, or I'd have had to answer her and then she would have known by the way I spoke that I had my mouth full. The taste of the Vicarage's dry bread was better than Gran's bread and butter, even when that was thick with butter.

16

I used to be frightened of going through those trees after I'd gone through the Vicarage gate when I went to fetch Mam after school in the winter and it was starting to go dark. They were like the trees in the graveyard at that time. But I'd be okay once I was past the bend in the path and I could see the light in Canon's study. I wasn't frightened then.

It was different in the summer. Dew, I remember once, there was no school one afternoon and I'd gone to the Vicarage and been allowed to go round the front and play with a little boy who had come there to stay. He called Canon uncle, and he spoke English. Dew, he was a nice little boy, with black hair, and it was shiny, and there was a nice quiff in it. And he had big black eyes, and his face was white, white as chalk, and he had little velvet trousers that showed half his legs, and white stockings, and slippers on his feet, not hobnailed boots like me.

That's why I was afraid of trampling the grass at the front outside the window when I was playing bat and ball with him, because I had hobnailed boots and the grass looked just as though Mam had been ironing it, not like the grass in Owen Gorlan's field. Dew, I said to myself as I played with him, I'd like to have manners like him. But I must have been a good boy, because I was allowed to go inside with him through the glass door at the front and sit at the table with him to have tea after taking my cap off. Afterwards, the two of us went to the Vicarage Garden to scrump gooseberries.

Ceri, Canon's daughter, caught us scrumping the gooseberries. She suddenly walked out from the middle of the flowers in the greenhouse, without us seeing her until she was right beside us. And I blushed right up to my ears and didn't say anything, in case I got told off, and then the little boy said something in English that made her burst out laughing. Oh, she had the nicest face I'd ever seen. I'll never forget it as long as I live.

How old is Ceri, Canon's daughter, Mam? I said when I'd gone home.

Oh, about eighteen, Mam said.

And I went to the bedroom and lay on the bed and cried because she was so old.

When I saw her that time, she didn't have a hat on, and she had the fairest of fair hair, and the sun was shining upon it, and there was a flower from the greenhouse fixed on the side of her head, and two long plaits of hair, with pink ribbons in them going down her back. She had a pink frock with all sorts of colours in it, like there were in the window of the greenhouse with all the flowers. And when she bent down to speak to us, with her chest in full view, there was a smell of scent everywhere, and I started shaking like a leaf. I told myself I'd never scrump gooseberries again, or go scrumping apples with Huw and Moi, or swear or do any kind of mischief. Nothing except think about Ceri.

Mam couldn't understand why I was walking so fast with the paper bag on the way home that night. And I didn't touch the meat or the crusts either. I just wanted to hurry home so I could go to bed and dream about Ceri. But I cried myself to sleep in the bedroom after Mam had said that Ceri was eighteen and too old for me to be her sweetheart.

But I'll pretend that she isn't so old, I said to myself before I went to sleep. And she must like me because she didn't tell Canon that me and the little boy had been scrumping gooseberries.

Dew, I don't know what Canon would have said either. He could be a wild one sometimes. I saw him in a rage once, but I don't know what about, and I didn't tell anyone because I was such good friends with him after he gave me that sixpence for not being able to read. But he wasn't in the same kind of rage as Price the School used to get into. Dew, I got a shock, too. It was a moonlit night just like tonight, and I'd gone to the Vicarage late to fetch Mam. That's how I saw him after going through the gate and up the path, they hadn't pulled the blind down on the study window, and that's where he was.

I went up very quietly behind the tree to peep in through the window, shaking like a leaf in case I got caught. He was walking backwards and forwards. Backwards and forwards without a pause from one end of the study to the other and beating his head with his fists. And if you'd seen his face! His eyes were flashing like lightning and his white hair was all over the place, not combed like it usually was. And that

18

scar by his mouth looked as though someone had just put a hot poker on it.

He was on his own, but his lips were going as though he was having a hell of a row with someone. I nearly had a fit when he came up to the window and looked out, frightened that he had seen me. But his eyes didn't look as though he was looking at anyone, only as though they were full of lightning flashing, although it was a fine moonlit night, except that the trees made it dark. His lips were still moving when he came to the window. But I couldn't hear anything, I could only see him, as though he was saying Strive ye for salvation through Godinjesuschrist. But maybe it was something else he was saying. The minute he turned his back to the window, I flew from behind the tree to the back door.

What's the matter with you, sweetheart? said Nell after she'd opened the door and given me a piece of bread and butter by the fire. You're as white as chalk. Have you seen a bogeyman?

No, course not, I said, wolfing down the bread. It's old women like you that see bogeymen.

But as I was sitting on the chair counting the tiles and thinking about Huw and Moi and me dirtying them by playing London on them, the three of them were sitting at the table talking very quietly about something.

I didn't say anything about it to Mam on the way home, and luckily I didn't dip into the paper bag because Mam didn't seem tired, like she usually did. And she was talking to me just as though I was a man and understood everything.

Do you know what those old devils in the Village are saying now? she said as we reached the gate into Lôn Newydd.

No, Mam, I said.

They're saying that God's to blame for the war. And a lot of them Church people too. There was a terrible atmosphere in the Vicarage this afternoon. Some of them went to see Canon to tell him they weren't going to go near the Church again until the war stops.

They're never saying that, Mam.

19

Yes, really, and Nell was saying it's that devil from The Blue Bell who's behind them.

Who, Johnny Beer Barrel's Dad?

Yes, the old good-for-nothing. Him and Johnny Williams the Barber. But they weren't with the gang who went to the Vicarage. The two old scoundrels are leaving it to other people to do the talking. While they're hiding behind a beer barrel, no doubt.

I bet they are too, Mam.

Yes, and they'll both be at Communion on Sunday as bold as that bloomin' Grace Ellen. But they really caught it from Canon in the Vicarage. Dew, he gave them a right telling off, Gwen said. Gwen had been listening to him lay into them when she took the tea in. Dew, you should have heard what Canon said to them.

What did he say, Mam?

Oh, nothing. Never mind what he said. Put the key in the lock. Dew, this washing's heavy tonight. I'm nearly dropping.

And she didn't say anything else after we went into the house, just told me to hurry up and have supper and go to bed so she could get on with the ironing. And I went, still thinking about Canon reading the riot act to those people, and about him reading it to himself when I was peeping through the study window, and promising to half kill Johnny Beer Barrel in school the next day cos his dad was telling the people in The Blue Bell that God was to blame for the War.

Maybe that's why Price the School never went to The Blue Bell at playtime again after that day when Canon came to School to say that Little Bob School had been killed in the War. Dew, I'll never forget that day. It was after playtime and Price the School had been in The Blue Bell and his face was red but he was in a really good mood too, and he didn't cane anyone.

He was busy telling us about the Germans cutting off women's breasts with swords and slicing little babies up the middle when Canon came past the Graveyard window and in through the door. And he went to sit quietly at the desk without Price hearing him come in and put his flat brimmed hat down on the desk and sat in the chair and wiped the sweat from his forehead with a big, white handkerchief. Price didn't know he was there even though no-one was paying attention to the lesson cos we were all looking at Canon. Price finally turned round when he heard him cough.

Then he stopped talking about the Germans and walked very slowly to the chair where Canon was sitting. Canon was twice as tall as Price the School when he got up from the chair, and the two of them talked together for ages and ages, with Canon holding Price's hand with his own right hand and with his left hand on Price's shoulder. And we didn't understand what the matter was until Canon sat down and wiped the sweat from his forehead again, and Price the School walked slowly back to us and said that Little Bob School had been killed by the Germans.

But what frightened us was seeing him fall to his knees on the floor and put his hands together as though he was going to say his prayers. And his eyes were closed and tears were rolling down his cheeks. Dew, I'll never forget what he said, either. I went straight home from school and I didn't move from the house until I'd learned every word, and Bob Milk Cart gave me sixpence the next Sunday at Sunday School for reciting them all the way through without a single mistake.

God who is my refuge and my strength, said Price with his eyes closed and the tears pouring, a very present help in trouble. Therefore will we not fear, though the Earth be removed; and though the mountains be carried into the midst of the sea; though the waters thereof roar and be troubled; though the mountains shake with the swelling thereof. There is a river, the streams thereof shall make glad the city of God: the holy place of the tabernacles of the Most High. God is in the midst of her; she shall not be moved: God shall help her and that right early. The heathens raged, the kingdoms were moved: he uttered his voice, the earth melted. The lord of hosts is with us: the God of Jacob is our Refuge. Come, behold the works of the Lord. What desolations he hath made in the earth. He maketh wars to cease unto the end of the earth; he breaketh the bow, and cutteth the spear in sunder; he burneth the chariot in the fire. Be still and know that I am God; I will be exalted among the heathen, I will

21

be exalted in the earth. The Lord of hosts is with us. The God of Jacob is our Refuge.

I was beginning to feel ill as I listened to him. Aw it's a shame, isn't it? I said very quietly to Huw, who was sitting beside me.

Yes, Huw said, but how can he cry with his eyes shut?

I don't know, boy.

Me neither.

Little did we think, Huw and me, that that would be the last time we'd see Canon alive. He wasn't in Church the next Sunday, nor the following Sunday, nor the Sunday after that. And on the Tuesday after that, we were looking at him in his coffin.

The coffin was in the study over there, but it was daylight and the sun was shining when we walked with the Church Choir through the Graveyard to the Vicarage, and once round the coffin and then back from the Vicarage to the Church and the Graveyard along Post Lane here. His mouth was shut tight, just as it always was after he'd finished preaching hellfire in the pulpit, or at choir practice.

Dew, I wish I could have come with you to the funeral, said Moi when we told him how he'd looked in his coffin.

But Moi was at chapel so he wasn't allowed to come. Only the choirboys were allowed to go.

Mam was right too when she said there'd be no scar on his mouth in Heaven. There was no sign of it on his mouth when I looked at his face as I passed by the coffin in the study.

Did you see that scar that was usually by his mouth. Huw? I said.

No, said Huw.

Me neither.

It died with him, I suppose, Huw said.

But talking about Mam. Dew, I thought she was going to go out of her mind that day when Little Owen the Coal shouted through the door, as he passed, that Canon had died in the Vicarage. And somehow, she was never the same after that. She never went to the Vicarage again to wash for Hughes the Parson who came there after him.

But the strange thing was, Canon never knew about John

Elwyn, Ceri's brother, dying, and John Elwyn never knew about Canon dying. It was on the Friday that Canon died and it was on the Friday that a telegram came to the Vicarage to say that John Elwyn had been killed by the Germans, just like Little Bob the School, and they were both the same age and just as good friends as Canon and Price the School were.

But everyone at the funeral knew, of course, that Canon and John Elwyn had died at just about the same time. And so we felt as though we were burying them both together, except that John Elwyn wasn't there. And when they put the gravestone up, John Elwyn's name was on it underneath Canon's name, exactly as though he was lying there with his father.

Dew, I felt sorry for Ceri at the funeral, with some strange man holding her arm and her crying her eyes out. But I couldn't see her face because she had a big, black veil hiding it, and she was holding her handkerchief underneath that to wipe her nose.

They've put the blinds down or I'm sure I'd be able to see Azariah Jenkins in his study from here. I wonder if he's walking backwards and forwards and going on at himself like Canon was all that time ago?

No point bothering to go over Stables Bridge even though it is moonlight. There's no sign of Moi and there's no light in the house. Dew, his Uncle Owen's ghost might come to meet me if I go that way. I'd better whistle as I pass Stables Bridge, and I'd better keep to Post Lane.

3

TO THINK THERE was a time when I didn't know where Post Lane went after it passed the end of Black Lake. Emyr, Little Owen the Coal's Big Brother was the first person I remember walking as far as the end of Black Lake, but he didn't carry on any further cos they found him there on his knees, with his shoes off and his feet all blistered, crying and shouting for his Mam. Huw and me couldn't understand what was the matter with him, and Moi was only pretending to understand, that's for sure, or else he would have told us.

Em was always scrubbing the doorstep when we passed Mount Pleasant on our way to School in the morning, and then he'd go into the house with the bucket and slam the door.

Why does he talk like a woman, d'you think? I said to Huw as we went by.

I don't know, said Huw.

Nor me, neither.

Perhaps he really is a woman, said Moi.

Shut up, you fool, said Huw. He'd be a she, then.

They say he dresses up like a woman when he's in the house on his own, said Moi, and puts curling pins in his hair and paints his face red and things like that.

No, who told you that? we both said together.

I heard Uncle Owen telling Mam the night Em got sent home from the Quarry for crying and not being able to do his work. But Jesus, you'd never think he was a woman if you heard him swearing at his Mam.

Get away, we said, does he swear at his Mam?

Oh yes. We hear him sometimes at the end of the Terrace at one o'clock in the morning. And the sound of a big fight there sometimes when Owen comes home drunk from the The Blue Bell. I heard them at it myself one night last week. Owen ran out after him shouting: Leave her alone, you devil, or I'll stick this knife into you, and chased him all the way down the street.

That was the night he went missing, wasn't it Moi? said Huw.

Who, Em? Yes, it was last Tuesday night.

It was a moonlit night just like tonight and everyone had gone to bed except Little Will Policeman's Dad. It was hearing him knocking Next Door, to ask Ellis, David Evans' brother, to come and help him look for Em that made me get up and go to the door to see what was going on. When I saw the Policeman standing at Next Door's front door, I went straight back to the bedroom and started getting dressed and putting my shoes on.

What's the matter? Where are you going? It's not time to get up yet, said Mam, half asleep.

Just into the street to see what's going on, I said quietly.

Is it that bloomin' Emyr at it again? said Mam. Don't go too far with them, mind. And she turned over on her side and fell back into a deep sleep. I went out very quietly, closing the door behind me and taking the key with me so I could get back in again when I came home.

There was Little Will Policeman's Dad in the doorway talking quietly with Ellis Evans. We'd better take a rope with us, said Ellis Evans, we might need it.

Yes, bring a rope, said the Policeman. We'll go over to Mount Pleasant first in case he's come back. All the others are waiting at the Crossroads.

Can I do anything, Ellis Evans? I said, with one eye on the Policeman.

Bed's the place for you at this time of night, he said.

But I followed them, and when we came to Mount Pleasant, the Policeman opened the gate and knocked on the front door. There was no answer until he knocked again.

Who the devil is it now? came Little Owen the Coal's voice. Get to Hell with you whoever you are.

Get yourself down here, Owen, said Ellis Evans, or you'll be in the Lockup. The Policeman wants to see you.

Go to the devil, came Owen's voice again.

Did Emyr come back? said the Policeman through the keyhole.

No, and the bugger won't, neither, came Owen's voice.

We're going to search for him with a rope, said Ellis Evans.

Well, if you see him, hang him to Hell. Now get back to your beds and get to sleep and let other people do the same, for God's sake, came Owen's voice. Let him drown or hang himself or whatever the Hell else he likes.

He's been drinking, said Ellis Evans.

Yes, leave him, said the Policeman. We'll carry on.

And we didn't hear a peep out of Owen's Mam. She must have been sound asleep.

And who was standing at the end of the Terrace with his hands in his pockets but Moi. How did you get out, Moi? I said.

Oh, Mam didn't mind cos Uncle Owen's with the men going to search for Em, said Moi.

Do you think Huw will be able to get out?

I don't know, boy.

Nor me, neither.

But who was there at the crossroads with the others but Huw. About a dozen men had turned up with it being a fine moonlit night, and the metalling was shining on Lôn Newydd. And everyone was talking and some were smoking and waiting for the Policeman to give them their orders. Hughes the Curate was there, and David Evans Snowdon View, and Little Harry the Clogs and Will Ellis Porter and Moi's Uncle Owen and Ann Jones the Shop's brother and David Jones the Keeper and Frank Bee Hive, as well as Ellis Evans and the Policeman and one or two others we didn't recognise.

Now then, lads, said the Policeman, we'll split into two groups. Ellis Evans will go with one group up the Waun, over

26

Pen y Foel to Pen Garnedd then come down Allt Goch to the end of Black Lake. I'll go with the other group over the Braich and up Post Lane and along the Riverbank, and we can all meet by the end of Black Lake. If Ellis Evans' group finds him, Ellis Evans can bring him to the Lockup, and if our group find him, I'll do the same, and everyone is to come back here to the Crossroads by five, find him or not.

He went to the Sheep Field to try and hang himself last time, said Frank Bee Hive.

Yes, we all know that, said the Policeman, but he's not gone there tonight. Mister Hughes saw him setting off in the opposite direction, and he could only be making for the Waun or the Braich that way. Now, everybody to his group and let's be away, or it'll be daylight. You three go home. Bed's the place for you, so you can get up for school, he said to us.

Yes, you go back to bed like a good boy, Moi, said Moi's Uncle Owen.

So we stood by the Crossroads for a bit to let the two groups go on ahead to the Waun and the Braich.

Hadn't we better follow them? I said. I'd like to see them catch Emyr.

Yes, we'll go, said Moi.

Only a bit of the way then, said Huw, or I'll get a hiding from Mam when I get home.

Which group shall we follow? I said.

I don't want to go up the Waun to Pen y Foel, said Huw.

Alright then, said Moi, we'll go up Post Lane past the Vicarage and Stables Bridge.

Dew, what if we meet him coming the other way on Post Lane?

Shut up, you fool, I said, we won't see him.

If we do see him, we'll whistle for the others and run home, said Moi.

Dew, I've never been out as late as this, said Huw. Where do you think he went, lads?

I don't know, boy, I said.

Nor me, neither.

27

There are lots of places for him to go if he wants to kill himself, said Moi. If it was the middle of winter, he'd only have to go out like Moi Ffridd and walk up past the Waun onto the side of the Foel and lie down in the snow till morning.

He can't do that on a fine night like tonight, said Huw.

Or if he wanted, he could climb up Pen Ceunant and throw himself head first into Man in the Moon Lake, said Moi. There's no bottom to that one.

And I didn't say anything, I just thought, and let the other two talk. Cos every time anyone mentioned Man in the Moon Lake, I thought about Mam singing in the kitchen while she did the ironing, and me in bed with tears rolling down my cheeks as I listened to the sad song.

On an ancient clifftop lonely
der-dum-der-dum dark night
sat a pure young maiden
der-dum-der beautiful sight
She gazed down far below her: a maelstrom whirling near:
a stranger's face she saw there:
then fainted she from fear.
Awoken from her fainting
still wild was she with fright:
eyes wild and ever-flashing
like sword blades in the night:
der-dum-der-dum-der-dum-dee der-dum-dee let me fly:
der-dum-der-dum-der-dum-dee I'm fated 'fore daybreak to die

Dew, I was sorry for that girl, and frightened that Mam would stop singing before she was saved by her sweetheart or whoever he was. And sometimes, I'd go to sleep in the middle of the song and wake up in a sweat as I was starting to fall from Pen Ceunant into Man in the Moon Lake while I was trying to save the girl.

Huw was saying to Moi: Why do people hang themselves, d'you think?

Because they're out of their minds, of course, I said.

Lor, it must hurt when the rope squeezes round your neck, said Huw.

No, it doesn't hurt much, said Moi.

Hey, how do you know?

It's easy enough to hang yourself if you want to. Just hang a rope with a noose on it over a branch or something and stand on a rock or something, and put the noose round your neck and jump off the rock. I tried it, just for fun, in the toilet at the bottom of the yard once, just to see. I put a rope with a noose on it behind the door and put the noose round my neck. I didn't jump off anything, I just crouched down and let it squeeze for a bit. It's easy enough.

Lor, your Uncle Owen would have battered you if he'd caught you, said Huw.

He would, said Moi.

Then we walked along Post Lane for a bit without anyone saying anything, except that Huw in the middle was whistling 'All Through the Night' very quietly. I was looking at the moon until we came to the bend at the bottom of Allt Braich.

Bloody Hell, watch out lads, said Moi, suddenly stopping dead in his tracks. Huw and me stopped too, startled. Come to the side of the wall and hide, he said, ducking down at the side of the wall, and we went after him and crouched down too.

What's up, Moi? I whispered.

Come behind this bank, hurry up you fools, and lie down flat and listen.

And there we were, the three of us, lying behind the bank round the corner at the bottom of Allt Braich when we heard something jumping over the wall into Post Lane and the sound of someone walking quickly up the middle of the Lane in big, hobnailed boots with something loose on one foot. He was coming closer and closer, and I was shaking like a leaf, and the three of us were waiting for him to come round the corner.

And what did we see coming round the bend but Emyr. He was in the middle of Post Lane, walking quickly and taking tiny little steps as though he was wearing a skirt that was tight round his knees, with his chin sticking out and his eyes staring up Post Lane. He had his hands stuffed up his coat sleeves as though he was an old lady wearing a muff. There was a strange smile on his face, and he was sticking his tongue out, and he looked like a dog who'd been killing sheep. I nearly choked trying holding my breath as he went past.

We'd better whistle three times and run home, said Huw after Em had vanished from sight up Post Lane and we were sitting on the bank.

No, better not, said Moi. The Policeman's group will be getting to Post Lane in a minute. They're sure to catch him.

No chance of that with him walking so fast.

Ah, but he'll be getting tired, for sure.

It was me who said: We'd better go back now, and Huw and Moi said Alright then. So we set off without saying anything else, back up Allt Braich and down Post Lane to Stables Bridge.

Uncle Owen's with the Policeman's group, said Moi. He'll tell me and Mam the full story when he gets home. And I'll tell you the full story on the way to school tomorrow morning.

This morning, I said.

Oh yes, quite right, this morning, said Moi, laughing as he turned to go over Stables Bridge. Good night, lads.

Good morning, Huw and I said.

Oh yes, quite right, good morning.

Maybe Ellis Evans' group will catch him, I said to Huw as we were approaching the Lockup. It'll be me who gets the news then, from Next Door, to tell you on the way to school, if I see Ellis Evans Next Door before he goes to the Quarry.

But it was the Policeman's group that caught Em on Post Lane by the end of Black Lake. And it was from Moi that we got the story about him on his knees by the side of the lane, with his shoes off and his feet all blistered and crying and shouting for his Mam. They made a stretcher with two poles and Hughes the Curate's overcoat, and carried him all the way down Post Lane and took him to the Lockup.

And Little Jini Pen Cae was missing that night too, although nobody knew. And Moi's Uncle Owen was saying that Em had taken her with him to the Woods on Allt Braich. It was in the Woods they found her next day, anyway, sleeping like a top beside a tree stump. We never saw Em again until that day

30

when Owen's Mam took us into the house to see him lying on the sofa in his coffin with his mouth wide open.

Old Em used to love taking little girls for a walk and lifting their skirts up, said Moi.

Poor old Em. It was right here that we saw him coming round the corner, behind that bank on the side of the lane. And it must have been about this time of night, too, a fine moonlit night like tonight. Good God, watch yourself in case there are any little devils behind that bank round the corner, watching you and thinking that you've gone out of your mind. Have a good look to make sure as you pass. I'm sure that if Em had looked properly that night, he would have seen us. But Em was staring ahead up Post Lane the whole time. Dew, I'll never forget his eyes. They looked as though they were seeing and listening at the same time.

What was he seeing, I wonder? If he'd turned his head to look to the left side, he wouldn't have seen anything but that bank with the gorse flowers on the side of the Braich. Maybe he saw a rat running along the top of the wall, like that one we saw once. He couldn't see anything on this right side either, just the Quarry slate tips shining in the moonlight through the branches of the trees. There's the odd squirrel in these woods too. He could have seen one of those. He'd have to have looked over the top of the wall to see the salmon leaping in the River. But he didn't look over the wall. He was looking ahead all the time.

He must have been able to see a long way from here too. Post Lane goes straight for a long way here after coming round the turn. It goes straight almost as far as the end of Black Lake. He was looking like this, with his eyes closed a little bit. I can't see anything except Post Lane all white with the River shining over there alongside it. There's nothing else then except a mountain on each side and lots and lots of shadows at the far end of Post Lane, and those go further away still as you walk on. Dew, I couldn't keep looking like this for long with my eyes half-closed. It hurts too much. Old Em's eyes must have been hurting that night, if he wasn't seeing any more than I'm seeing. What was it he could see, I wonder?

31

But maybe he was listening with his eyes. Maybe he could hear the Voice. What Voice, you silly fool? There's no Voice. But there was a long time ago, though. Don't you remember Mam telling the story of Will Starch Collar hearing it on Stables Bridge one night? And it was with his two eyes that he heard It, anyway.

I was sitting in the chair by the fire, trying to learn Bible verses, with Mam ironing a starched collar on the table. I remember what the verse was, too:

Behold, I shew you a mystery; We shall not all sleep, but we shall all be changed. In a moment, in the twinkling of an eye, at the last trump: for the trumpet shall sound, and the dead shall be raised incorruptible, and we shall be changed. For this corruptible must put on incorruption and this mortal must put on immortality.

I'd repeated it to myself scores of times, and I was watching the iron in Mam's hand going to and fro over one starched collar after another as I tried to say the verses without looking. And so I'd remember certain words like, say, trumpet, I just thought about the Salvation Army Band. And the words Put On Incorruption and the fact that Mam was ironing made me think about Will Starch Collar playing the trombone with the Salvation Army Band on the street corner by the Lockup every Saturday night.

Just for fun, to try and make Mam laugh, I asked: Is that Will Starch Collar's collar, Mam?

No, indeed. They're all Canon's collars. You know full well, she said, and she didn't laugh.

I was only joking, I said.

You get on with learning those verses. You should be ashamed of yourself making fun of a man like Will Starch Collar. If you studied your Bible half as much as Will Starch Collar does every day of his life, you'd be a much better boy, instead of going off to make mischief every night with that bloomin' Huw.

And she carried on ironing without saying anything else for a little while, until I was in the middle of saying: Behold, I shew you a mystery . . .

He wasn't always a good man like he is today, either, you know, Mam said. Who? I said.

Will Starch Collar. He was a bad old devil a long time ago, in the bloomin' Blue Bell drunk every night, and swearing and fighting in the street and going to sleep under the hedge till morning instead of going home to White Houses. And his Mam keeping the lamp lit and staying up all night waiting for him. A real handful he was when he was a young lad.

How did he become good, then?

Heard the Voice he did. Move your feet in case I burn you, said Mam, as she put a fresh block of hot metal from the fire into the smoothing iron with the tongs.

What Voice?

Never mind what Voice, she said, going back to her ironing.

You don't remember those days, chick. You hadn't been born. It was the time of the Revival and lots of people were hearing the Voice every night. It was in Salem Chapel that most of them heard It. But there were some who heard It by the side of the Foel, and some on Allt Braich, and others on the Riverbank, and some were just walking along Post Lane and some were just lying in bed.

Really?

Yes, really. There was a strange atmosphere round here in those days. But Will Starch Collar was the only one who saw and heard the Voice at the same time.

Saw the Voice? How could he see a Voice?

Well, he'd been in The Blue Bell drinking all evening one night, and he was going home rolling drunk, staggering from one side of the road to the other along Post Lane past the Lockup. And when he turned off Post Lane to go home across Stables Bridge to White Houses, he suddenly felt terribly ill, and put his head over the side of the Bridge to be sick. And when he'd finished throwing up and was still looking down into the River, what did he see but a great wheel of fire, whizzing round and coming along the River and up the side of the Bridge. And when it came over the Bridge wall and stopped by the side of Will Starch Collar, although the old devil wasn't wearing a

33

collar or tie at the time, the wheel of fire started to speak to him.

Will, you old sinner, the Voice of the wheel of fire said to him, haven't you been saved yet? Do you know where you're going? Do you know you're going to Hell, headfirst into the middle of the fire and brimstone, to damnation for all eternity? And Mam lifted the iron from the table and turned it round in her hand to show me how the wheel of fire was speaking.

Poor Will, she said. He was leaning on the wall of the Bridge and shaking like a leaf and staring like an idiot at what he was seeing. Then he started shouting: What shall I do? Oh, dear Mam, what shall I do? Then the wheel of fire answered him, saying: Repent, sinner, Repent. And then the wheel started to whizz round and went back over the Bridge wall and down to the River and went out.

Old Will went back home to White Houses as sober as a saint, and where do you think they saw him next?

I don't know. Where, Mam?

On his knees in the Sinners' seat in Salem Chapel, shouting with all his might like a madman: Salvation is like the sea, ever rolling to the shore. He never went near the old Blue Bell again, anyway, and instead of sleeping late and missing his shift in the Quarry and going about without changing his clothes after Quarry Supper, he had a clean collar every night and a black tie to go to the Fellowship Meeting and the Prayer Meeting in Salem Chapel.

When the Salvation Army came here, he went to join them. And for ages afterwards, he used to tell the story of the wheel of fire on Stables Bridge in his Saturday night sermon outside the Lockup. He never tells it now, not since he's started playing that old trombone in the Salvation Band.

Mam was good at doing impressions of people. This is how he used to finish his sermon, she said, and held the iron up in her hand and raised her voice to sound like Will Starch Collar outside the Lockup.

I am Saul of Tarsus, he used to say, said Mam. I am Saul of Tarsus. I have seen the light of eternal salvation shining upon me. But it wasn't on the road to Damascus that the light of eternal salvation shone upon me. No, my dear people, it was from a wheel of fire on Stables Bridge on the road to White Houses. And it shone on me, me who was not ashamed to sit among those who mocked the Lord in The Blue Bell. Take warning from Saul of Tarsus before it is too late.

But everyone called him Will Starch Collar, said Mam.

Dew, Mam was on good form that night, and I was rolling about laughing and having great fun listening to her take the mickey out of Will Starch Collar.

Did you hear the voice anywhere, Mam? I said.

I don't know, she said. No, not as far as I know, love. I was a young girl at the time, you know. But I've heard a great many strange things since then. Yes, by God. Have you finished learning your verses?

Just about, I said. But I'd forgotten all the verses by the time I went to bed, and I couldn't sleep for the life of me until Mam came to bed. Then all night I kept seeing the wheel of fire whizzing round and hearing the sound of firecrackers just as though it was Bonfire Night.

4

ONE THING'S FOR SURE. I won't lose my way on Post Lane tonight, like I did the day we went to pick bilberries. Moi wasn't with us that day. He was in bed cos he'd caught a cold when Little Owen the Coal took him with him to catch salmon and made him stay out all night without his overcoat, looking out for Jones the Gamekeeper.

They only caught two, Moi told us the week after. What good were two salmon, he said. With me having to go to bed for a week and not being allowed to go out to play or go bilberry picking with the lads to Pen y Foel?

We'd said the night before that we'd meet at the Crossroads at five o'clock in the morning, everybody with his pitcher and his tuck box. Everyone was there before five except Huw, and I was feeling a bit uncomfortable cos all the others were girls except me. Mary Plums and her two daughters were there with enormous pitchers, not little ones like me and Nell Fair View and Kate White Houses had. We only had a little pitcher each cos we were only going to pick bilberries to take home. Mary Plums and her two daughters had big pitchers cos they were going to sell their bilberries when they came home and get a lot of money for them.

Come on, lad, I said to Huw when he arrived, we've been waiting for ages.

It's only five o'clock, said Huw, rubbing his eyes. Huw had a little pitcher too.

Come along now or the sun'll be up, said Mary Plums.

So we set off for the Waun the same way that Ellis Evans Next

36

Door's group had gone looking for Em, Little Owen the Coal's Brother. We'd asked Mary Plums and the others if we could go with them cos we didn't know the way to where the bilberries were on Pen y Foel. Mary Plums wasn't very keen at first.

You're too small, she said.

We're as big as your two girls, said Huw.

Alright then, said Mary Plums. But mind you'll have to walk sharpish and not go wandering off.

We will, I said.

We won't, said Huw.

Dew, it was cold after we passed Waun Farm, and we followed each other quickly through the Foel gate. Nobody was up yet at Waun Farm. But we woke one poor soul up when we made a noise squeaking through the gate. It was Charlie, Ellis the Waun's dog, who was there barking his head off, but he must have been tied up cos he didn't come after us.

When it started to get light and we'd been walking for a really long time, I thought we'd reached the top of the Foel.

No, you silly fool, said one of Mary Plums' girls who was in front of us, there's a long way yet. That's why Huw and me thought we'd reached to top, cos there was white mist around us, but the further we walked, the further the mist went, and the more mountainside was coming into view. We were always thinking we'd reached the top of the Foel, but we'd only reached the top of a small hillock and there was always another hill in front of us.

Dew, I'm nearly out of breath, said Huw behind me, and I started to slow down and Mary Plums and the others were getting further ahead of us all the time.

Come on you old slowcoaches, came the voice of one of Mary Plums' girls when they were just about to disappear from view over another hill, Mam'll send you home if you can't walk faster than that.

Come on Huw, I said to Huw. We mustn't dawdle any more.

And the two of us were puffing like steam engines. But when the next hill came into view, Mary Plums and the others were sitting on the top of it waiting for us.

They must be tired too, said Huw behind me.

It was great to have a break when we got to the top of the hillock and we sat down and relaxed and looked down the hill at the Village far below us, so far that it was nearly out of sight. There was smoke coming from every chimney and, on the other side, a wagon was moving on top of the slate tip in the Quarry.

What time is it, I said?

Half past seven, said Nell Fair View.

How much more walking have we got? Huw asked Mary Plums.

Only half an hour.

Are there a lot more hills?

No. There it is, Pen y Foel.

And when we looked up, there wasn't a bit of mist ahead of us, just Pen y Foel and the sky.

We're starting picking over there, said one of Mary Plums' girls, pointing out the distant spot to us.

We had to walk for about another half hour but it was great to be able to walk on the flat along the sheep track among the bilberry bushes, instead of walking where it was slippery all the time. And after reaching the best spot for picking bilberries, we all sat down and everyone opened their tuck boxes and took out some bread and butter. Huw and me had forgotten that we'd be thirsty and we hadn't brought a bottle of milk like the others had. But Huw had a drink from Nell Fair View's bottle and Kate White Houses gave me a little drink from hers.

Off you go now, everyone with their pitcher, said Mary Plums, and everyone went off to start picking bilberries.

Hey, you've been eating bilberries, said Huw after we'd all been picking on our own for hours, your mouth's all blue. And you've not even covered the bottom of your pitcher yet. Look, I've got mine quarter full.

I put some in a sandwich, I said. Dew, it was good too. Like bilberry pie.

Don't let Mary Plums see the bilberry juice on your mouth. She won't let the girls eat a single one.

I'll wipe my mouth, then.

No good, it won't come off. I fancy going over there to pick with the girls now. They're in the best place for bilberries.

Alright, I want to stay here. You go ahead.

And Huw went.

From where I was sitting I could see Post Lane a long way below me, and the River alongside it too. And motors going back and forth along it like ants, some going up to the end of Black Lake and others coming down into the Village. I'm sure, I said to myself, if I set off I could slide all the way down to Post Lane, except that I'd be going at a hell of a speed when I reached the bottom and I'd have no brakes, like Davey, Johnny Edwards Butcher's boy, when he went flying down Allt Rhiw on his bike and crashed into Bob Milk Cart's wagon and got a big dent in his forehead. I'd have a great slide down to Post lane if I had a brake, I said, and made another bilberry sandwich with the few I had left in the bottom of the pitcher. Then I'd be able to walk down Post Lane without having to go all the way down from Pen y Foel and through the Waun. I'd be home long before the others.

You'd think the sky would look so near from here, with us having climbed so high. But it didn't look close at all as I lay flat on my back, seeing nothing but blue sky without a single cloud to spoil it, and the sun hot on my cheeks. Dew, it must be great to be allowed to go to Heaven, I said. It's strange that I can't see Heaven from here or see an angel flying somewhere over there. That must be the underneath side of Heaven's floor and the floor on the other side must be blue too. Dew, it must have needed a lot of blue colour to make it all. Much more than Mam uses on washing day.

I couldn't understand where I was when I woke up, with pins and needles all through my arms after going to sleep with my hands behind my neck. There were clouds in the sky when I woke up and I felt a bit cold. I'd better go over to the others now, I said, taking hold of my pitcher and getting up. Hey, they were all over there but now there's no sign of any of them. What will I do, now? I said, beginning to get frightened. I started to make my way through the bilberry bushes but I just couldn't find the sheep track and I couldn't see anybody anywhere.

Dew, you would have been scared if you'd been me. Walking for miles, seeing nothing but bilberry bushes everywhere and the air like a sea swirling all around me. My heart was beating like a drum and I started running and then I stumbled on a rock or something and fell into the middle of a bilberry bush and lost my pitcher. I was too frightened to get up for ages afterwards and I was shaking like a leaf.

And then I thought about Huw. Maybe he's lost as well, I said. And that made me get up and start walking about very slowly and looking everywhere to see if I could see anyone. But I couldn't see anything except bilberry bushes and the sky, and I was frightened of shouting or whistling cos it was all so quiet.

Then I carried on very slowly not looking at anything except the ground to see if I could see the sheep track. Dew, I was glad when I found it right in the middle of the bilberry bushes.

But I just couldn't find the way to go. This is the way back, I said. Then no, it's this way. And I stood like that for ages, trying to make my mind up. In the end, I held my hand out and spat on it then gave the spit a slap with my finger. The spit went to the right. That way, I said, and started to hurry along the sheep track.

After I'd been walking for ages, the sheep track began to go downhill. Those are the hills we climbed, they must be, I said.

What will Mam say about me losing the pitcher? I've got one piece of bread and butter left, I can eat that when I get down to the next hillock. Where's my tuck box? Damn, I've left that in that bilberry bush too. I haven't got any bread and butter now. Dew, I'm thirsty. It's a pity I didn't bring a bottle of milk to drink like Nell Fair View and Kate White Houses. Where are they now, I wonder? Back at home, no doubt, with pitchers full to the brim with bilberries. Dew, that Mary Plums is good at picking bilberries. Did you see her picking them with two hands at once, kneeling in the bilberry bushes with her pitcher there by her knees, and she didn't lift her head up once to look round until it was time to eat our bread and butter. Dew, that bread and butter would be nice now. Maybe I'll catch them up when I get to the top of the next hillock down there. I hope old Huw's with them and he hasn't got lost like me. Dew, my mouth's dry, just like Em, Little Owen the Coal's Brother, when he was lying on the sofa. A cup of tea would be nice now.

I was talking to myself like that all the time as I walked down the sheep track until I came to the top of the next little hill hoping that I'd see Huw and the others going down ahead of me. I nearly had a fit when I got to the top of the hill. What did I see instead of Huw and the women ahead but Post Lane still far below and a lot of rocks to one side of it and a big lake without any sun on it on the other side. That's Black Lake, it must be, I said, and I knew then that I should have gone the other way and that the spit had lied to me. I'll never believe what Moi said, about spitting on your hand if you've lost your way, ever again. Good job I don't want to spit on my hand now, I wouldn't have enough spit in my mouth to do it. Dew, I'm thirsty.

I thought for a minute that I'd better go back the other way along the sheep track, but when I turned my head to look, I didn't see anything behind me but the hill going right up to the sky. But this path is bound to go down to Post Lane, I said, and I'll be okay once I get to Post Lane.

It was getting much warmer down here too and the sun had come back onto Post Lane although it hadn't reached up the mountainside to the spot where I was or to Black Lake. But I didn't expect to see it there cos that's what Ellis Evans Next Door told me the morning after they'd found Emyr. The sun never shines on Black Lake, he said, that's why they call it Black Lake, you see. Mam will have a fit when I tell her I've been near Black Lake. Hurry up, or you never will be near it, I said, and down the hill I went as fast as I could.

There was a farm by the side of Black Lake on the flat bit before you came to Post Lane. I'll go and ask if I can have a drink of water, I said. Maybe I'll get a drink of milk and water mixed from them cos I'm nearly dying of thirst.

I stood by the gate for ages, scared to go to the door cos there was a dog barking in the back somewhere. I was about to risk opening the gate when a lady came to the door. She had a kind face with blue eyes, white hair and rosy cheeks. I was just starting to open the gate.

What do you want, my boy? she said.

A drink, please. I'm nearly choking, I said.

Good Lord, you do look tired, come here and have a glass of buttermilk. Would you like some bread and butter with it?

Yes, please, I said, and went through the gate and stood by the door and she was talking to me from the kitchen.

I've been picking bilberries on Pen y Foel and I lost my pitcher and my tuck box and I lost my way and came down to here, I said.

You poor little thing, said someone else in the kitchen.

There you are, you drink this and eat this bread and butter. You'll be fine afterwards. Sit here. Where do you come from?

From the Village.

You've got a long way to go on Post Lane.

Thanks very much, I said, taking the big piece of buttered bread and the big glass of milk and going to sit on the slate seat under the window. I'll be fit to walk miles after this.

Then while I was busy drinking, who should come zooming round the end of the house but the dog who I'd heard barking in the back. Leave the little boy alone, Toss, said someone from the kitchen and Toss stopped dead when he saw me sitting on the slate seat. He was a big sheepdog with eyes the same colour as glass eyes. He growled a little bit to start with and I was frightened that he was going to bite me. So I made a sort of kissing sound with my mouth.

Come on then, Toss, I said, and when he heard me say his name he wagged his tail and opened his mouth and let his tongue dangle out the way dogs do when they're laughing.

Come on then, Toss, I said again, and broke off a piece of my bread and put it beside me on the slate seat. Then he came up very slowly, wagging his tail and took the piece of bread from the seat. When I broke off another bit for him, he took that from my hand and then put his front feet on my knees and began licking my face. We were great friends in no time and after we'd finished eating the bread and butter, we played throw the stone in the field for a while. Then I took the empty glass back to the house and knocked at the door, and Toss ran inside to the kitchen.

There you are, said the rosy-cheeked lady as she took the glass. You look a bit better now, my boy. Go straight home now or your Mam will start to worry about you.

I'm going. Thanks a lot. How old is Toss?

Fourteen.

Lor, he's older than me. Good afternoon.

Close the gate after you, she said.

It was great to walk along Post Lane after walking on grass all day cos it was a flat road for the best part of the way. It was there that they found Emyr on his knees, must be, I said as I was passing the wall by the side of Black Lake.

Dew, it was hot after I'd walked about a mile and I took my coat off and walked in my shirtsleeves. The sun had melted the tar on the lane and my hobnailed boots were beginning to stick to it every step I took. I'll take them off, I said, and sat on the grass by the side of the lane and stuffed a sock into each shoe and knotted the laces together and hung them round my neck over my shoulders.

I was okay then, and could go like the wind and the tar was a warm slush under my feet until I got to the bottom of Allt Braich. I'd better put my boots back on now, I said, in case anyone sees me. So I sat down behind the bank where we saw Em going past. And I remembered that Em had his boots off, as well, when they found him. But there weren't any blisters on my feet, though.

It was lucky that I got home when I did, or there would have been a hell of a fuss just like when Em went missing. I'd only just gone over the doorstep, and I hadn't even had a chance to sit down or say anything except Hello Mam when there was a knock at the door. And who was there when Mam went to the door but Huw gasping for breath and stuttering.

I-I-I, he was saying, looking as though he was about to have a fit, and then he saw me behind Mam making faces at him to shut his mouth.

What's the matter with the boy? said Mam. But Huw just stood there staring at her.

I've run up the hill and got out of breath, he said at last.

Well, come in and sit down then, said Mam.

I couldn't bear watching Huw sitting there scowling at me as Mam was pouring tea out of the teapot. Poor Huw. He just didn't know what was going on.

Why were you running up the hill, Huw? said Mam.

It was me, I lost my way, I said.

Lost your way where?

On Pen y Foel.

Damn this old teapot.

And lost the little pitcher, I said.

You little monkey. Come and eat your food then you can go and get washed. You look like a chimney sweep. Would you like a cup of tea, Huw?

No thanks, said Huw. I'd better nip off and tell Mary Plums and the others or one of them's sure to tell Little Will Policeman's Dad.

Yes, you go in case he gets a search party out, said Mam.

Yes, I'll go now, said Huw, and he legged it out of the door and ran off down the Hill. I didn't see him again that night. We were both too tired to go out to play, and Moi was in bed with a cold.

Nothing, I said, washing myself in the bowl at the back when Mam asked what had happened on Pen y Foel. Nothing apart from me going to sleep cos I was tired, then waking up and going to look for the little pitcher and not being able to find it or the tuck box. I lost them both through walking about trying to find the little pitcher and then I started walking along the sheep track to try and find them but I just couldn't. Lor, I'd better go home, I said, or Mam will be worried. I'll go home along Post Lane so I can be home quicker and I ended up going down to Black Lake.

Black Lake? said Mam from the kitchen. You weren't near Black Lake? she said, very slowly as though she was frightened.

I got a glass of milk and some bread and butter from the lady at the farm, I said, combing my hair in the mirror. They've got a dog and he's fourteen. His name's Toss.

I was just trying to keep talking in case she was cross with me. But when I went back to the kitchen, spotlessly clean with my hair combed, she took hold of me and lifted me up in her arms and gave me a great big kiss on my cheek that lasted for ages.

My little chick, she said, I don't know what I'd do if you went missing. And the tears were rolling down her cheeks. I didn't understand what she was crying about.

Someone knocking at the door made her put me down and who was there when Mam went to the door after drying her eyes but Mrs Evans Next Door, Ellis Evans' wife. Hello stranger, said Mam, cos Mrs Evans hadn't been in our house for two nights. Come in, Grace Evans.

Only for a minute, she said, closing the door behind her. My kettle's nearly boiling.

Sit by the fire, said Mam. What is it?

I thought you wouldn't have heard with you being out all day, said Mrs Evans, sitting down in the chair after I'd made room for her and gone to sit on the fender to listen. You'll be surprised when you hear about Lisa.

Who, Lisa Top House? I said, not catching what she'd said.

Yes, the poor creature, said Mrs Evans without looking at me.

Oh, that one, said Mam, collecting the crumbs from the tablecloth and folding it, and pretending that she didn't want to know anything about Lisa Top House. But I knew she was all ears, really. Things hadn't been too good between her and Lisa since that day Lisa burst through the door and told Mam to stop gossiping about her.

Some people do nothing but gossip all day while other people have to work hard to earn a crust, Mam said to Mrs Evans.

Poor Lisa's been very lonely, said Mrs Evans.

What's she been up to now, then? said Mam, sitting down and starting to poke the fire.

Nothing, said Mrs Evans, but you'll be surprised when you hear.

Hear what, Grace Evans? Mam said, but don't tell me another of those bloomin' stories they're always telling about Lisa, no matter how much truth there is in it. Anyway, she won't be able to say it's me who's gossiping about her this time.

But Grace Evans was in a good mood. You listen now, she said, and gave Mam a friendly prod. She was always much more familiar with Mam when she was in a good mood. I say, this boy's all ears on the fender. Now listen so you'll hear. And she gave Mam another prod.

Hear what?

And Mrs Evans said: Ellis had just finished his Quarry Supper and he was sitting in the chair by the window putting his glasses on to see what the *Herald*'s got to say this week, the gossip and that. That's the first thing Ellis does after Quarry Supper every Monday night, goes and sits in the chair by the window and puts on his glasses to read. And no-one can get a word out of him once he settles down with his paper until it's time for him to go to bed. This cat's better company than you when you've got your head in that old paper, I always say to him. But Ellis always was a great one for reading.

Yes, well then? said Mam, what were you saying about Lisa?

Well, yes my girl, said Mrs Evans, putting her hand on Mam's knee. That's what surprised me about Ellis tonight. He'd just sat down and put his glasses on when he suddenly got up from his chair and took his glasses off to look out of the window. What's the matter with you, Ellis? I said, surprised.

Dew, he said, with his glasses in his hand, and turned to look at me like a man in a dream. I must be failing, and that's a fact, he said.

Failing what, Ellis? I said. Failing to read?

Dew, he said again, still looking right through me. I'll never believe it wasn't him.

Who wasn't him? I said.

Him who passed by the window just now, said Ellis.

Who did you think it was? I said.

Humphrey, he said. But I must be wrong, surely, he said, and put his glasses back on and sat down.

Which Humphrey? I said.

He was very much like him, anyway, he said and picked up his paper again.

Which Humphrey do you mean, Ellis? I said again.

Humphrey, Lisa's husband. He was just like him. And he had a big bag on his back going up the Hill.

Good Heavens, I wonder, I said, and I ran through the door to see.

Surely it wasn't him, said Mam.

Wait a minute, said Mrs Evans, and began rocking in the chair. When I went to the door, who was standing at the top of the Hill in front of Lisa's house but the man Ellis said was the image of Humphrey. There he was knocking at the door and the next thing we heard was Lisa's voice shouting loud enough for the whole street to hear her. My darling Humphrey, my dearest love, she said, tell me, is it you? Come home to your Lisa? And we could hear her shouting and crying until we went back into the house.

Well, you don't say, said Mam slowly, staring into the fire.

And Mrs Ellis got up from the chair. I just thought you'd like to hear, she said. Good Heavens, my kettle will have boiled dry, I'm sure. Ellis won't notice anything. He never does when he's got his nose in that old paper. And she shot through the door like a squirrel.

Why are you crying again, Mam? I said. Aren't you pleased that Lisa's husband has come back from the sea?

Hush you fool, I wasn't crying, she said, drying her eyes with her apron and still staring into the fire. I was just thinking about your dad.

5

SEEING MAM'S EYES all red when I woke up the next day made me remember it was Good Friday. Talk about miserable, that was the most miserable day of my life, until tea-time anyway. And even then, after tea, nobody came out to play, cos Huw had gone away with his Mam somewhere, and Moi was in bed with a cold.

I went gathering sticks for Mam to the Woods Behind the Garden after breakfast and even then I had a headache. Mam had told me not to be long cos she wanted me back to look after the house so she could be at Church by twelve o'clock. She went to Church at twelve o'clock every Good Friday and stayed there till after three in the afternoon.

I didn't tell her about the headache, I just said Alright Mam, I'll come back in time to look after the house and then I can chop sticks in the back. I never used to say anything to her about it being Good Friday, not since that time ages ago when she told me why she always went to Church at twelve and stayed there till after three.

Why do you always go to Church at twelve? I said to her that time.

Cos it was twelve o'clock when they crucified Jesus, she said.

I'd learned the story in Sunday School about Jesus being crucified, but it didn't sound the same when Mam told it.

So why do you stay in Church till after three?

To suffer with him, she said. He took three hours to die, you know, after they knocked nails into his hands and feet with a hammer.

48

They never did that to Him. It's not true.

It is, really.

Do you want me to come with you to Church to suffer with you?

No chick, you're still too young. You can come when you've been confirmed.

What do you do to suffer there for three hours, Mam? Sing psalms?

No. I say psalms. Nobody sings on Good Friday. Nobody except those bloomin' Chapel people.

I didn't ask her anything else and she didn't tell me anything else. But every Good Friday after that, for ages, I'd always stand still wherever I happened to be when the midday shot was fired in the Quarry, and I'd start thinking about them knocking the fiᵣst nail into His hand with a hammer, two of them at the tops of two ladders, one holding His arm and the other knocking the nail in.

I remember one Good Friday, we'd gone to the Sheep Field to gather pignuts and we were still at it when the midday shot went.

What's up? said Moi when he saw me stop gathering nuts and just stand there without saying anything.

I'm remembering Jesus being crucified.

It's his Mam, she's a very religious woman, you know, said Huw as I carried on standing still. She goes to Church every Good Friday.

Would you like someone to knock nails into your hands with a hammer? I said to them. Course you would.

Nobody did that, you stupid fool, said Moi. They just crucified Him.

But that's what crucifying is, though. And he didn't scream or anything, he just prayed, while they were busy knocking the nails in.

Dew, I'd squeal like a pig if anyone just stuck a pin in my hand, said Huw.

I can stick a pin in my hand without shouting, said Moi. Have you got a pin? I'll show you.

49

And when he'd got a pin from Huw, Moi started sticking it through the skin on the palm of his hand as though he was darning a stocking, and then the point of the pin came out again from under his skin. And he didn't make any sound at all.

It's fairly easy. You just have to hold your breath.

I forgot all about the story of Jesus then, until Mam came home from Church. But on this particular Good Friday, I was on my own in the back chopping sticks when they fired the midday shot in the Quarry and I had a hell of a headache. And when I stood still, the longer I stood the more I thought about people hammering nails, and my head hurt as though someone was knocking nails into it, so I had to go inside and lie down. And when I lay down, I started shaking like a leaf and there was cold sweat on my forehead, and I began to think all kinds of things. Dew, I really wanted Mam. I'll go and fetch her from the Church, I said, and got up and started walking slowly through the door. I was nearly crying I was so ill and I wanted to be sick but I couldn't. I was feeling so weak, I went down the Hill holding onto the wall in case I fell over. Dew, it was a fine day, too. The sun was hot but I was covered in cold sweat and my eyes were hurting as though someone had gone behind them with a hot pin and was plucking away at the roots. Oh, and the pain in my head.

Luckily, the gate to the Graveyard was open. I could never have opened it, being so weak. And it looked a hell of a long way from the Graveyard gate to the Church door, although really it was only a few yards. I was hoping that Mam would be sitting in our old seat near the door so I could call to her quietly and ask her to come out cos I was ill. But I felt sure she'd have gone to a new seat halfway down the aisle. Dew, I just can't go any further, I said.

So what did I do but lie down on the grass at the side of the pebble path. Just to rest for a while, I thought, before carrying on to the Church door. I began to think all sorts of things when I lay down, I was looking at the Church tower and the stones in the wall and the slates on the roof. Dew, it must be old, I said. I'm sure it looked nice when it was a new Church, before the

50

wind and the rain and the frost and the snow and the heat from the sun dirtied it. It's like that stone hen that used to be in our house before if got broken to bits, the one with all her chicks around her, and they were stone as well. But my headache was too bad for me to look for long, and my eyes hurt.

I got a shock when I woke up and saw where I was lying. I wasn't on the grass but on somebody's grave that the grass had grown over. There was a wreath of white flowers that had gone yellow in a glass pot with rusty wires around it, and the pot had just about disappeared from view in the grass and the weeds. I couldn't read anything on the gravestone except In Loving Memory and there were pictures of oak leaves. My eyes were hurting too much to read any more and I just wanted to close them. So I did close them, and started to think what if I died right there on Good Friday.

It'd be a lot better than somebody knocking nails into your hands and feet, I said. But Dew, my head feels as though somebody's knocking nails into that, though. And it would be great afterwards to be raised from the dead on Easter Sunday just like Jesus, and creep about the village without anyone seeing me, and not tell anyone except Mam and Huw that I'd been raised from the dead until Ascension Day. And then go up to Heaven like a balloon from the top of the Foel. I wouldn't like to go and leave Mam and Huw though. Dew, my head hurts.

It was just like being raised from the dead when I woke up, too. I didn't have a clue where I was. But then I realised I was lying in bed in Mam's bedroom, lovely and warm. And then Mam came into the room with a cup of tea and a hot-cross bun on a plate, and started laughing so much she nearly spilt the tea on the bedclothes.

What are you laughing at, Mam? I said, beginning to laugh with her.

Seeing your face when you woke up, chick, she said. You looked just like you'd come back from the dead.

Lor, I said after drinking my tea and wolfing the hot-cross bun, it's great to wake up without a headache. It's just like being raised from the dead.

And that's what made me suddenly remember lying on the grave in the Graveyard. How did I get to bed, Mam? I said.

You were asleep in the Graveyard when we came out of Church, chick, and I carried you home and undressed you and put you to bed. And you didn't wake up once.

Dew, I was ill.

You're alright now though, aren't you, chick?

Yes. Any more hot-cross buns? What time is it?

Only half past five, said Mam, going out of the room to bring me another hot-cross bun. I jumped out of bed and started to get dressed, full of the joys of spring. Talk about me getting better, dew, she was better too after being in Church and suffering all afternoon. She wasn't the same woman she was earlier on. She was laughing at everything I said to her and going all around the house, into the back kitchen and the front room and the loft, singing all the while. I could easily have forgotten it was Good Friday except that the oven was full of hot-cross buns. I was just about to remind her that it was only those bloomin' Chapel people who sang on Good Friday, but then I thought maybe I'd better not.

She called from the front room: Don't you eat too many of those hot-cross buns, you little guts, or you'll be sick again.

I won't, Mam.

Go out for a walk up the Hill. It'll do you good.

Alright then, I said, and I put my cap on and out I went.

And when I got to the top of the Hill, who should be sitting out in the sun under the window of Top House but Humphrey, Lisa Top House's husband, who'd just come back from the sea. When I saw him, I thought about Huw Pen Pennog going around the village balancing his basket on his head without touching it and shouting: Herrings ... Fresh ... Just out of the sea. I'd never seen Humphrey before cos it was a very long time ago when he went away. Before I was born, Mam said. He must be a very tall man, I said to myself, looking at him as I passed by, cos as he sat there with his knees pulled up to his chest, his knees were right up in the air and his bare legs were showing at the tops of his socks, and his face was yellow like a Chinaman's.

Who's lad are you? he said as I went past, with a voice that frightened me.

I'm from the house down there, I said pointing.

Come here. Come and sit here so I can see you.

He had blue eyes exactly like the lady at the farm near Black Lake, but his cheeks were yellow instead of red, and wrinkled like brown paper when it's been used to wrap a parcel up.

When I sat down, he went into his waistcoat pocket and pulled a small box out and put it into my hand.

Open it up and see what you can hear, he said.

But when I opened the box, there was nothing in it, and I couldn't hear anything.

Can you hear anything?

No.

Put it up to your ear. Can you hear anything now, then? he said, and his blue eyes looked as though they were laughing at me. I didn't say anything, I just nodded my head and listened, and something from inside the box was playing ding dong ding dong somewhere far far away, as though I was listening to the Church clock striking when I was on the top of the Foel, except that the bells in the box were playing a proper tune. Dew, it was a nice tune, too.

Lor, it's good isn't it? I said to Humphrey. Can I have another listen?

You have to close the lid first.

Would you like to keep it? he said after I'd listened again.

Dew, yes.

Well, stick it in your pocket.

Lor, I said, and put it in my coat pocket.

Then he went into another waistcoat pocket and pulled out something that looked like a knife. Watch now, he said, as he held the knife in his right hand and pressed on the handle with his thumb. And the blade jumped out of the handle like a jack-in-the-box. Watch again, Humphrey said then, and after looking at me to make sure I was watching, he stabbed himself in the left hand with the knife and I saw the blade go right into the palm of his hand.

Dew, you're hurt, I said, expecting to see blood. But there was none. And Humphrey was rolling about laughing at how shocked I was. Cos the blade hadn't gone into his hand at all. It had gone back into the handle.

Hey, you're a good 'un, I said laughing. And he had all sorts of tricks in the pockets of his coat and waistcoat.

He was showing me another one, how to kill six Germans with a matchbox and six matches, when Lisa, his wife, called him to come into the house. Just for a minute, Lisa said.

You wait here, I'll be back in two minutes, said Humphrey and off he went into the house.

I sat down where I was and took the little box out of my pocket to hear the tune again. Dew, I thought the world of that box, and I'd hear its faraway bells ringing at odd times for days after I got it from Humphrey. I could hear them without opening the box or putting it near my ear, especially in bed every night, just before going to sleep.

Anyway, I'd put it to my ear after Humphrey went in to see what Lisa wanted, and I was still listening to it after the bells had stopped ringing. But cos I was sitting under the open window, I could also hear Humphrey and Lisa whispering to each other. They were speaking too quietly for me to hear what they were saying, but as I was listening to see if the bells were still ringing, I heard Lisa say Mam's name. I couldn't make out what she was saying to Humphrey. Something not very nice, I'm sure, I said to myself, cos Mam and Lisa had fallen out. Maybe she was telling Humphrey not to give me anything and to send me home. And I was frightened of Humphrey coming out and saying he wanted the box back. Dew, it's a pity they've fallen out, I said, keeping a tight hold on the box in my pocket.

But Humphrey was laughing his head off when he came back out of the house to crouch down under the window again. I don't really remember how he killed the Germans with the matchbox. He opened the box then stuffed a match in each side between the box and the lid and put another match lengthways between them. Then he lit another match on the side of the box and held it under the match that was lengthways between the other two until that one caught light and jumped into the air. And the match that jumped was the German that had been killed.

That's how it's done, you see, he said, and laughed at me with his blue eyes. That's how to kill the buggers.

Then Humphrey looked up and down the Hill to see if anyone but me could hear him. Do you swear? he said.

No. I only say damn when I lose my temper.

Good lad, said Humphrey, and spat on the floor between his knees. Don't you ever learn to swear.

And instead of asking for his bellringing box back, what did he do but go into his waistcoat pocket again and pull out the knife and give me that as well.

There's a sharp edge on it, you know, when you've learnt how to open and close it, he said. Let me show you.

And he put my thumb on the handle and pressed until the blade jumped out.

You can carve anything with this, you know.

And he showed me how it closed. He just put the tip of the blade on the ground and pressed. And it went into the hilt and made a click.

Lor, you're a kind man, I said.

Is your Mam at home? Humphrey said suddenly, after I'd put the knife away in my other coat pocket.

Yes.

What's she doing?

She was making the bed when I came out. I've been sleeping in it all afternoon.

I like a little nap in the afternoon too, said Humphrey, lighting up his pipe and spitting.

I wasn't well, that's why I was sleeping. I felt ill after Mam had gone to Church, and I went down to fetch her, and fell asleep in the Graveyard when I lay down waiting for her to come out. And she saw me lying across the grave asleep, and snoring as though I was drunk, and carried me home and put me to bed, and I stayed fast asleep all the time. Dew, your tobacco smells nice.

Eh, d'you think so, lad? Humphrey said slowly as though he

55

wasn't really listening to me. And she carried you all the way home, did she?

Yes, really, I said as the smoke swirled around Humphrey's face. I like the smell of your tobacco.

And Humphrey puffed away for a while just like the little train in the Quarry. Then he turned round, still in his crouching position, till he was facing me.

Look, he said, tapping his pipe against the wall and putting it in his trouser pocket. Will you ask your Mam to come here for tea on Sunday afternoon with Lisa and you and me.

She won't come, I said sadly.

Why won't she come?

They've fallen out, and they don't speak each other.

Oooh, said Humphrey, his voice going up and down. Is that so? What did they fall out about?

Er, it was your wife saying that Mam was gossiping about her, I said with both hands in my pockets keeping a tight hold on the knife and the bellbox. But Humphrey was roaring with laughter as he got up from his crouching position and I got up with him.

Then he bent down and whispered in my ear: All women like to gossip, you know. And this here Lisa's as bad as any of 'em.

Dew, Humphrey was a tall man.

Now, he said in his normal voice, after he'd straightened up and I had my neck bent back so I could look at him. You make her come on Sunday afternoon, and you as well. And tell your Mam, he said, going into his pocket and pulling something out in his fist. And tell your Mam, my lad, that Humphrey, Lisa's husband gives her this as a present.

And before I knew what he was doing, he'd put a ten-shilling note in my hand.

Lor, you're the kindest man in the world, I said, and ran like the wind down the Hill to tell Mam.

Yes, really, I told her again when she refused to believe me the first time. Lisa and Humphrey want you to come.

Alright then, said Mam slowly, the two of us will go there for tea on Sunday. Fair play to old Humphrey.

56

You should have seen Lisa Top House this afternoon, Ellis Evans' wife told Mam when she popped in on her way home from the Bridge Shop at teatime the following day.

Mam and I were just coming back from the Village, we'd been doing the Saturday shopping, and I had ninepence in my trouser pocket. I went with Mam to the Village every Saturday afternoon and I never came home with less than ninepence. Mam would stop to talk to all sorts of people in the Street or in John Jones's Shop where you bought the blue stuff for washing, or in Roland Jones Early Potatoes' Shop or in the Pork Shop.

And whoever she spoke to would say Dear me, this little boy's growing. Or dear me, how old is he now? Or well I never, doesn't time fly, how old are you now, lad?

And I was sure of a penny from everyone, and I got as much as eighteen pence sometimes on Settling-up Saturdays and I used to carry the shopping basket up the Hill for Mam when it was heavy.

She was a hell of a show, my girl, said Mrs Evans and gave Mam another prod on the knee.

What was the matter with her, then? said Mam.

She was a hell of a show, said Mrs Evans again—and I didn't understand and wanted to know what sort of show—she had false teeth and a hat and a brand new fur, and she was walking down the street as if she owned the whole Village, with Humphrey holding her arm.

You don't say, said Mam, surprised. Funny we didn't see them and we were in the street all afternoon. Poor Lisa.

Poor Lisa what? said Mrs Evans. You'll see. She's so grand these days after getting Humphrey back, she's turning her nose up at all of us.

Then you should have seen Mrs Evans' eyes open wide when I said: Mam and me are going for tea at Top House tomorrow.

She gave Mam a strange look and her eyes, after opening wide, half closed again. I thought you and Lisa weren't friends, she said.

But Mam didn't say anything, she just stared into the fire.

Humphrey Top House invited me, I said. Look what I got from him.

And I got the box of ringing bells from the dresser and opened it and put it against Ellis Evans' wife's ear. Can you hear the bells ringing? I said.

No, she said, and got up to go.

And I got this off him, too, I said, and pulled the knife out of my pocket. But Ellis Evans' wife didn't want to hear or see anything.

I'd better not gossip any more, she said, making for the door. Those sailors are terrible old so-and-so's. And my old man will go mad if he doesn't get his tea. Ta-ta now.

And away she went, and when I came back after seeing her to the door, there was Mam still staring into the fire. But she was laughing her head off by then.

What are you laughing at, Mam? I said.

I can't wait to see Lisa in her false teeth, she said.

6

I WAS THE FIRST one to arrive at Church the next morning. Dew, it was a fine Sunday morning, too. The sun was shining on the clocktower and on the stone angels in the Graveyard and the bell started to ring as I went through the gate.

Ho-lycherubim-and-Se-ra-phim we sang at the tops of our voices. It was a morning for singing, too. Huw and me always sat next to each other in the choir and we liked Communion mornings better than any other Sunday morning even though we hadn't been confirmed. We liked watching the people coming up in a long line to kneel before the Altar, and seeing who was there and who wasn't.

But we had to watch what we were doing in the choir, too, because Frank Bee Hive's dad on the organ could see us through the mirror near his head even though he had his back to us when he was playing it. But we could do lots of things under our surplices without Frank Bee Hive's dad seeing us.

It was only the once that I played pinch under our surplices with Huw, and I wouldn't have done it that time either if I'd used my eyes before we started and seen that Huw's Mam never cut his nails for him. Hughes the Parson had just started praying and we were at it playing pinch.

You give me your hand under my surplice and I'll give you my hand under yours, said Huw. You can pinch me and I'll pinch you. And the winner will be the one who can stand it the longest without shouting Ow.

There we both were, looking into the mirror on top of the organ with our faces like wood, then bending our heads to pray, and pinching each other's hands like hell under the surplice. I kept it up without so much as wrinkling my nose until about half way through the prayers, when Hughes was talking about Angels and Archangels and the entire Company of Heaven. And then I shouted Ow very quietly and Huw bent down pretending to pick up a hymn book and turned his head to look at me.

I've won, he said.

When I looked at the back of my hand, it was pouring with blood and a piece of skin was hanging off. I had to put a hankie round it and keep it in my pocket till the end of the service. The scar's still there.

Dew, there's some good singers in this morning, said Huw after we'd sat down after singing Holy Cherubim that Sunday. I haven't seen it so full for ages and ages. Do you know why it's so full?

No.

People want to know what Hughes the Parson is going to do with Grace Ellen Shoe Shop after her having that baby. Where's your Mam? She's not in her seat.

She goes to Eight o' clock Communion, then stays at home to make the dinner.

We didn't say anything else for a while cos Frank Bee Hive's dad was eyeing us in the mirror, and Hughes the Parson and Hughes the Curate were walking up to the Altar. After they'd gone, we went down on our knees to pray. Before I joined the choir, when I used to sit in our seat with Mam, we didn't have to kneel down, just bow our heads. But in the choir we had to kneel down because everyone could see us.

I used to love it during prayers. Ceri, Canon's daughter used to sit among the altos on the opposite side from me, by the organ, and I could watch her through my fingers without her knowing, and think all sorts of things about her. Ceri was still in black and wore a veil on Sundays, cos it was just a year since Canon had died. Perhaps she wasn't too old to be my sweetheart either, I told myself. In ten more years, I'll be twenty and she'll only be twenty-eight. Maybe she'll marry me then if I ask her.

Come unto me all ye that labour and are heavy laden, and

I will give you rest, came Hughes the Parson's voice from the Altar.

She hasn't got a sweetheart yet, anyway, I said. A funny thing as well, her being such a pretty girl. But she's sure to be too upset about Canon to think about a sweetheart now. But by the time she's twenty-eight, she'll have stopped grieving for him, I'm sure.

Therefore with Angels and Archangels and with the entire Company of Heaven we laud and magnify thy glorious Name, we all said together.

Then Hughes the Parson and Hughes the Curate were kneeling before the Altar with their backs to us, and we were all still on our knees, and Hughes the Parson was praying on his own: We are not worthy even to gather the crumbs under thy Table, he said, as I peeped through my fingers at Ceri and thought about the bags of crusts and bread and butter and left-over meat that Mam and me used to carry from the Vicarage ages ago when Canon was alive and Mam used to do the washing there.

Here they come, said Huw when we'd sat down and Hughes the Parson had finished praying and got the bread and wine ready. The men and women of the choir and the boys and girls who had just been confirmed would walk to the Altar first, and then the people would start to come up from the Floor.

I bet Mary Plums is the first to get here from the Floor.

I bet John Morris Gravestones is first, I said.

Mary Plums and her two daughters had set off from their seat on the right-hand side of the Floor, and John Morris was coming up from the left-hand side. And when they got to the lectern they were just about level pegging but then Mary Plums took a giant stride forward and pulled her two girls with her in front of John Morris.

I won, said Huw.

Mary Plums' two girls had just been confirmed, that's why she wanted to be at the front with them. And who came behind them and John Morris but Kate White Houses and Nell Fair View. They'd just had Bishop's Baptism as well.

Do you remember Ascension Day last year? said Huw out of

the side of his mouth. He was trying to attract Kate's and Nell's attention but they both kept their eyes on the Altar straight ahead of them until they'd gone past us. Huw and me were being confirmed next time.

By this time, the people from the Floor were streaming up in a long line to the Altar. Little Will Policeman's Dad was next in line, wearing his own clothes.

I'd never think he was policeman, said Huw.

Nor me neither.

Next came Ann Jones the Shop, leaving her brother in the pew cos he'd not been confirmed before going to America. Huw and me looked down at our hymn books while Ann Jones was coming up. Lisa Top House was behind her, really standing out in her new clothes and, like Ann Jones, she'd left Humphrey in his pew cos he'd not been confirmed before he went to sea.

Dew, what if old Will Ellis had a fit now, said Huw when Will Ellis Porter came up behind Lisa Top House. But old Will was in good spirits and gave Huw and me a sly wink as he went past.

Little Harry the Clogs came behind him, with his hands stuffed into his sleeves and looking as though he was laughing hee-hee-hee to himself, and taking tiny little steps so that it looked as though he was running to the Altar instead of walking.

Next came Little Jini Pen Cae's dad, Owen Gorlan, David Evans, Johnny Edwards Butcher, Little Owen the Coal's Mam, Jones the New Policeman looking more like a policeman in his own clothes than Little Will Policeman's Dad did in his, and Ellis Evans' wife, and lots of others that we didn't know very well. Frank Bee Hive and Ellis Evans Next Door and Price the School had gone up with the first lot cos they were in the choir.

By now, there was a row of people filling the railings in front of the Altar and Hughes the Parson was going along the row with Hughes the Curate. Hughes the Curate was putting the bread in everyone's hand and Hughes the Parson was going behind him with the cup of wine.

The body of our Lord Jesus Christ der-der-der-der, Hughes the Curate said to everyone. The blood of our Lord Jesus Christ der-der-der-der, said Hughes the Parson after him.

Huw and me used to look at their shoes while they were kneeling down to see who hadn't had them soled. Will Ellis Porter's and Little Harry the Clogs' would always have holes in the soles; but it was Lisa Top House's fox fur that attracted our attention that morning. We could see it's head laughing at us from her shoulders with its black eyes shining like stars.

Do you think it was Charlie, the dog from Waun Farm, that caught that fox on Lisa Top House's back? said Huw.

Quiet, you fool, I said. Humphrey her husband brought it back for her from across the sea. Mam and me are going there for tea this afternoon to get the full story.

Oh yes, of course, said Huw. Jesus! Look who's coming.

By now, the back end of the queue was just arriving at the Altar, and we'd thought that Mrs Jones the New Policeman, the one who was a maid at the Vicarage when Mam used to go there, was the last. But who suddenly got up from her pew at the back of the Floor by the door, and walked up dressed to the nines with a white-spotted veil over her face but Grace Ellen Shoe Shop.

Who is it? I said before I saw who it was.

Grace Ellen Shoe Shop, said Huw. Do you remember seeing her in the Sheep Field with Frank Bee Hive ages ago?

Sure I do. When we were collecting pignuts.

Yes. Well, she's had a baby and nobody knows who the father is.

You don't say. But why not?

She won't tell anyone.

Maybe she doesn't know herself.

Maybe not. She used to go to the Sheep Field with somebody or other just about every night, said Huw.

Maybe it's Frank Bee Hive who's the father.

Shut up. His dad's watching us through the mirror.

By now, Grace Ellen Shoe Shop had come up and was standing on her own waiting for someone to get up after their Communion to make room for her by the Altar railings.

The body of our Lord Jesus Christ der-der-der-der, said Hughes the Curate. The blood of our Lord Jesus Christ der-der-der-der, said Hughes the Parson until everyone had got up from the railings and Grace Ellen Shoe Shop was there on her own, kneeling with her head bowed. Hughes the Parson and Hughes the Curate had gone back to the Altar and were standing with their backs to us, doing something with the bread and wine, but we couldn't see what it was they were doing.

Then Hughes the Curate came and said the body of our Lord Jesus Christ der-der-der-der and gave Grace Ellen a piece of bread and she cupped her hands and swallowed it and then put her head in her hands and prayed. By now everyone in the choir and all the people on the Floor were sitting in their seats and looking at Grace Ellen all alone there waiting for Hughes the Parson to turn round with the Cup and bring her the wine.

But Hughes the Parson didn't turn round, he just stood right there with his back to us and his head bent backwards as though he was looking up at the angels and the picture of Jesus and his Mother in the coloured window above the Altar.

Grace Ellen didn't move from her knees for ages either, she just waited for the Cup with her head in her hands. In the end, when it was clear enough to everyone that Hughes the Parson wasn't going to turn round and bring the Cup to her, Grace Ellen got up and turned round and started walking back down from the Altar, with the eyes of everyone in the Choir and on the Floor upon her.

But you should have seen Grace Ellen. She was as proud as anyone in that Church. As she passed us, she took hold of the white-spotted veil on top of her hat and put it over her face and tied it under her chin. And instead of walking back to her seat, what did she do but walk down the middle of the Floor and turn left, and out she went through the door.

Dew, it's a shame for her, said Huw.

Yes boy, I said. But it's her own fault for going to the Sheep Field.

After she'd gone, everyone's eyes turned back to the Altar. Hughes the Parson and Hughes the Curate were there with their backs to us, still doing something with the bread and wine and still saying The body of our Lord Jesus Christ der-der-der-der and the blood of our Lord Jesus Christ der-der-der-der.

Watch Hughes the Parson as he swallows, said Huw.

And as he said it, Hughes the Parson began to drink from the cup and his head went further and further back until it looked as if he was looking at the roof with the cup upside down on his mouth.

I wonder if he'll be drunk now, I said to Huw.

No, course not. Communion wine isn't the same as the beer in The Blue Bell, you know. And he has to drink every drop that's left over once it's been consecrated.

Then the two of them, Hughes the Parson and Hughes the Curate, were still kneeling with their backs towards us. Our Fa-a-th-e-r, said Hughes Parson. Our Fa-a-th-e-r, we all said together in the Choir and on the Floor. And we said The Lord's Prayer together.

When Hughes the Parson got up and turned round, his face was as white as his surplice. And he was looking straight ahead as though he'd seen a ghost at the door, but there was nothing there.

Oh Lord and Heavenly Father, we said after him, although we be unworthy through our many sins to offer unto thee any sacrifice, we beseech thee to accept this our bounden duty and our service, while not weighing our deserts but forgiving our sins . . .

But by now I'd lost my place in the book and I was peeping through my fingers at Ceri and thinking about Mam making dinner. Meat and roast potatoes. I could almost smell them already and I was dying for the service to end so that I could run home up the Hill.

The peace of God which surpasseth all understanding, said Hughes the Parson at last in the Vestry. Amen, we all said, and then it was off with our surplices and cassocks on the pegs and out we went.

Are you coming to help me pump the organ for the English service this afternoon, Huw? I said when we got to the Grave-yard Gate.

Yes. And afterwards we'll go for a walk to the Sheep Field before tea.

Alright then, I said, and ran home up the Hill.

Dew, that smell's good, I said to Mam as I sat in the chair to watch her put dinner on the table. D'you know who was at Communion this morning?

No. Lots of people, I'm sure.

Yes. The Church was full. Lisa Top House was there with Humphrey, but Humphrey didn't come up to take Communion. D'you know who else was there?

No.

Grace Ellen Shoe Shop.

She never was. The dirty little madam. People like her aren't fit to take Communion.

She didn't get it.

But I thought you said she was at Communion.

She was, but she didn't get it.

Mam was putting peas on the plates with a big spoon, but she stopped and looked me right in the eye.

What do you mean, she didn't get it?

Hughes the Curate gave her the bread but Hughes the Parson wouldn't give her the wine.

You don't say. Mam was still looking at me as though she was in a dream. You don't say, she said again slowly, and went on putting peas on the plates.

It's a shame for her, isn't it?

But perhaps he was in the right, she said.

But why did they give her the bread but not the wine?

Well, that's what they do, you know. Come on now, to the table. I'm sure you must be nearly starving, and she changed the subject.

I didn't ask any more about it.

It was lucky that Huw came with me to help pump the organ for the English service that afternoon too. Little Owen the Coal had asked me to go instead of him cos he wanted to go catching rabbits with Owen Gorlan. I'd been in the organ pumping room once before, and that was with Owen, when he'd shown me how to push the blower up and down and make sure the organ didn't run out of wind. Owen would always come out of the room whenever it was time for the sermon and sit in the seat under the pulpit resting his head on his hand, listening. You can stay inside during the sermon in case people see you, Owen said to me that time.

And I said the same thing to Huw that afternoon. The English service was a right miserable affair. Only about a dozen people went to it. Mister Vincent the Bank and his wife and their little boy, Cyril, who was growing his curly hair just like a girl. They didn't understand Welsh, that's why they came. And because they came, that's why Mrs Ellis the Bee Hive and David Evans Snowdon View's wife and one or two others came, not cos they couldn't speak Welsh.

It was Hughes the Curate, not Hughes the Parson who took the service, and this was the first time he'd been in an English service. It was lucky that Huw had come to help too, cos the organ bellows were so heavy, I'm sure I wouldn't have been able to pump them up and down on my own.

Dew, Little Owen the Coal must be strong, I said to Huw when we were pumping away to Nunc Dimitis.

He is. Have you seen his muscles when he's in his shirt sleeves? Pumping the organ's good for building muscles, you know.

Yes, I said and took over the pumping from Huw. But that wasn't the only reason I was saying it was lucky that Huw had come with me.

You can stay in the bellows room during the sermon if you like, I told him when Hughes the Curate went up into the pulpit and was saying In the name of the Father and of the Son and of the Holy Ghost.

Alright then, said Huw. You go out.

Alright, I said, and I went out and sat in the seat under the pulpit and settled down to listen, with my hand under my head like Little Owen the Coal. Hughes the Curate spoke English just as well as he did Welsh, and although I did my best to listen to him, I was still thinking about other things. I only remember one word of that sermon, and the reason I remember it is cos I couldn't understand what it meant. Monotonousness was the word Hughes the Curate said, exactly as though he were speaking Welsh. Mo-no-to-nuss-ness, he said slowly.

Dew, yes, it was lucky that Huw had come with me. It must have been just about the time when Hughes the Curate was saying Monotonousness that I went to sleep. The next thing I remembered was jumping up in the seat when the organ started playing Awake my soul and with thy strength, and flying back into the pump room. And there was Huw pumping away for all he was worth and laughing his head off at me.

You're a fine one, he said.

Moi laughed his head off as well when Huw told him what had happened. After Church, I wanted to go the Sheep Field for a walk, but we didn't go.

There's nothing there on Sunday afternoon, you know, said Huw. The nuts aren't ready for gathering yet, and we couldn't gather pignuts anyway in these Sunday clothes. We can go and see old Moi in bed.

Alright then.

We've come to see Moi, said Huw after we'd knocked at the door and Moi's Mam had answered it with her hair in pins and looking as though she'd just woken up.

Come in, chicks, she said. Go up to him in the bedroom. I'll make a cup of tea in two minutes.

We were feeling more comfortable than the last time we were both there when Moi's Uncle Owen was alive, before he hanged himself, but as we were going up the stairs, Huw gave me a prod.

Look who's here, he said.

And there was Moi's Uncle Owen in a black frame on the wall looking at us, and his face was just like an angel's.

And I got a shock when I saw Moi in bed but I didn't show it.

Hello, how are you, old Moi? said Huw.

How are things? I said.

Hullo lads, said Moi, sitting up. I'm okay, you know, but Mam won't let me get up. She says maybe I can get up tomorrow after the Doctor's been, but that's what she said last time, too.

That's what you get for going to catch salmon with Little Owen the Coal, said Huw laughing. D'you know where we've been?

No. But I wish I'd been with you.

In Church pumping the organ for Little Owen the Coal cos he's gone catching rabbits with Owen Gorlan.

He's a great organ pumper, you know, said Huw and started to tell him about me going to sleep. Old Moi was helpless with laughter.

But even though we were laughing with him, I couldn't for the life of me take my eyes off Moi's face. Talk about eyes. His eyes were shining exactly like the eyes of that fox we saw on Lisa Top House's shoulder in Communion, and his face was all white like Hughes the Parson's after he'd refused to give the wine to Grace Ellen Shoe Shop, except that there were two red patches on Moi's face, one on each cheek. And then, suddenly, as he was laughing his head off, he started coughing like I don't know what.

Get me the pot from under the bed, Huw, he said between coughs. And Huw put his hand under the bed and pulled the pot out.

Hold it so I can spit in it, said Moi when he got his breath back.

Jesus, you're spitting blood, said Huw and the three of us stopped laughing, and Huw and me looked at the blood in the pot.

It's nothing, you know, said Moi when he stopped spitting and coughing and Huw had put the pot back under the bed. I always spit blood when I get a cold. D'you know who's coming to stay at The Blue Bell, boys?

Who?

Johnny Beer Barrel's cousin? said Huw.

Yes, but how did you know? said Moi.

I guessed. I've heard Johnny Beer Barrel saying that his cousin comes from the South and bragging that he's a boxer and that he could give anyone in the Village a hiding. How do you know, anyway? You've not been out.

Mam told me.

Then Moi's Mam shouted up the stairs: Come down now boys, and have a cup of tea.

You go, lads, said Moi. I'll see you tomorrow in School.

And we went downstairs to have a cup of tea with Moi's Mam.

We've been in Church, I told her. Pumping the organ in the English service for Little Owen the Coal.

Yes, you're good boys, she said. And Moi will be able to go to Church with you every Sunday when he gets better.

Will he really? I said.

Can he get up tomorrow? said Huw.

I don't know yet, till the Doctor comes.

We didn't say anything about Moi spitting blood.

Were you in Chapel today? I said.

No. I haven't been since we lost poor Uncle Owen.

You should have been in Church this morning, said Huw. Dew, I felt sorry for her.

Sorry for who?

Grace Ellen Shoe Shop. Hughes the Parson refused to give her Communion.

Really? He's a miserable old devil. Him and his Church. No, he can't go, now I think about it, Moi can't go to Church with you when he's better. Not while that old devil, Hughes the Parson's there anyway. Poor Grace. Ooh, it's an old devil he is.

And Moi's Mam was still cursing Hughes the Parson when we left.

Jesus, I nearly forgot, I said to Huw after we came out. Mam and me are going to tea at Lisa Top House's. I'll have to leg it. Ta ta now.

Dew, the weather was lovely when Mam put her best hat on and came with me to Top House. And you should have seen Mam and Lisa when Lisa opened the door. There they were, hugging each other and laughing and crying at the same time, and Humphrey was standing behind Lisa and making all sorts of faces at me, shutting one eye and sticking his tongue out and twisting his nose with his finger and thumb until I was rolling about laughing.

70

Dew, it was great listening to Humphrey telling wonderful stories at the tea table, and Lisa laughing at everything he was saying, and showing off her false teeth. And Mam was laughing too. And the door was wide open and the sunshine was streaming in. And there was all kinds of food to eat, and I was sorry I'd already eaten Sunday dinner at home. I nearly fell asleep in Church afterwards that Sunday night cos I'd eaten so much.

7

JOHNNY BEER BARREL's cousin was called Johnny, too, and so
we'd know which one we were talking about when he came to
stay at The Blue Bell, we called his cousin Johnny South. And
whenever anyone from the South came to the Village, everyone
would look at them in the Street as though they had horns
growing out of their head, and laugh at they way he spoke cos
their South Walian Welsh was so funny.

Jesus, the people in the South talk funny, don't they? said
Moi when we went to see him the following day. Pass me that
pot again.

And there was poor Moi, still in bed and still spitting blood.

And that was the last time we saw old Moi. The following
Sunday night, Huw called round and his face was like chalk.

Have you heard? he said at the door without coming in.

Heard what? said Mam.

Come in from the door Huw, I said. What's up?

Moi's dead, he said quietly.

Moi? No, you're telling lies Huw.

But I knew by his face that Huw was telling the truth. I just
needed to say something, just like ages ago when I used to whistle
as I went along Post Lane after dark, pretending that I wasn't
frightened of bogeymen.

And we were talking to him on Monday night, I said, as
though I still didn't believe it.

He was spitting a lot of blood that night, said Huw.

That bloomin' TB, said Mam. It takes young and old alike.

Then I started to cry like a baby. I couldn't stop for the life of

72

me, though I tried my very best to stop cos I was embarrassed with Huw and Mam watching me.

Moi and him were close friends, Huw said to Mam. But, of course, Huw was making excuses for me crying cos he was as close to Moi as I was. You never saw Huw crying like I did.

But Huw cried, too, at the funeral though nobody saw him that time except me. It was only one little tear that rolled down his cheek and even I wouldn't have seen that if he hadn't wiped his eye with the sleeve of his surplice, as we both stood with the choir at the graveside singing:

> My friends are homeward going
> Before me one by one
> And I am left an orphan
> A pilgrim all alone

That's what we sang at Griffith Evans Braich's funeral, and Canon's and all the others, too, but we were just singing cos we got tuppence for singing at those. It was different at Moi's funeral cos he was our friend and the words were true. I couldn't see anything when Hughes the Parson threw a handful of soil onto Moi's coffin after they'd lowered it into the grave with a rope cos my eyes were just like two windows after it's been raining.

But if you'd seen Moi's Mam after Hughes the Parson threw the soil onto the coffin. Huw and me thought she was going mad. She was stooping down on the other side of the grave, with two men holding her, one on each arm. And when the soil was thrown in, she let out a terrible scream just like when Moi's Uncle Owen was going to stick the knife in her neck ages ago, and she fell forward. And she would have fallen right into the grave on top of Moi's coffin if the two men hadn't kept a tight hold of her.

Dew, to think old Moi's lying there in a coffin with all that earth on top of him, Huw said when we went to see the grave the following Sunday morning, after the service in Church.

And he was talking and laughing in bed a week last Monday,

I said. Do you believe those things Hughes the Parson says about rising from the dead?

I don't know, boy. But Hughes the Parson doesn't tell lies, with him being a Parson and all.

He does worse things than tell lies, Huw. I'm sure Canon would never have refused to give the Communion wine to Grace Ellen Shoe Shop like Hughes the Parson did.

Dew, you're a strange one, Huw said.

But I just couldn't get the thought of Moi lying there out of my mind.

Do you think Moi will rise from the dead like Hughes the Parson says? I said to Mam that night. But Mam was tired and not in a mood to answer questions.

Go to bed now, chick, she said, so you can get up tomorrow morning. And don't worry about Moi. He's in a better place than you or me tonight.

But I could still see old Moi lying under the soil when I went to bed, and during the night too. And then I started dreaming. There was Moi in my dream, lying in bed in a grand room somewhere, smiling happily at me, with a lot of angels standing there and flying around him.

Dew, this is a fine place, he said when he saw me. But before I could say anything, all the angels took hold of his bed and started flapping their wings and making a terrible noise all through the place like the pheasants in the Sheep Field. And then all the angels and Moi's bed suddenly started to rise up and up they went through the roof, and Moi kept smiling at me till he went out of sight. And I didn't see anything else till I woke up at six o'clock to go and fetch the Tal Cafn cattle.

Moi would have been thrilled to bits to see Johnny South give Owen Gorlan such a hell of a hiding behind The Blue Bell. And I wouldn't have seen it if I hadn't seen Robin Gorlan when I was coming down from Pen y Foel after fetching the cattle.

Have you seen Johnny South? Robin said as we walked through the Potato Field after he'd pulled up some potatoes for me to take home.

Yes. He talks funny, doesn't he, Robin?

He's opened a boxing booth behind The Blue Bell.

You don't say, boy.

He has, really. And anyone, it doesn't matter who, can go there to learn boxing for a shilling a week. I went there with Owen the other night to see Johnny South go through his paces. Dew, you should see him. He's a good 'un, and no mistake.

Really?

Yes, really. He's made a big square ring in the stables of The Blue Bell, with rope railings all around it. And that's where the lads go every night to learn boxing. Johnny South calls them up one at a time and batters them, and he gets a good battering back sometimes as well. There's room for about twenty lads to sit on the seats around the ring.

Did he give Owen a hiding?

No. Wait till I tell you what happened. After we'd seen one round between Johnny South and Frank Bee Hive and Frank getting a hell of a belting, Owen and me went out. Then Owen went into the bar and I went into the Chip Shop next door. And when Owen came out of the bar, he was all mouth. The southern bastard, he said, I'll teach him to come up here showing off. Come back with me, Robin boy, and you'll see.

And did you go back there?

Yes, and when we got to the door, Johnny South was standing in the middle of the ring in his shorts and vest and wearing his boxing gloves. Now then, he said in his Southern Welsh. At eight o'clock next Tuesday, there'll be a special show here—Johnny South against whoever wants to challenge him, over three rounds. And if there's anybody here with a big enough punch to KO Johnny South, he'll get ten shillings for his purse.

Dew, you speak South Walian really well, Robin.

And Owen shouted from the door: Okay you Southerner, I'll see you next Tuesday. And everybody turned round to look at us. At eight o'clock, then said Owen, pretending to talk like Johnny South.

Taken, said Johnny in English, with a big smile on his face. He wasn't scowling like Owen was.

Next Tuesday, Robin?

Yes. And our Owen's asked Little Owen the Coal to be his second and they want me to help. And Johnny Beer Barrel will be Johnny South's second. Johnny South wanted three rounds but Owen insisted they made it four. So I'll have a chance to give him a proper pasting, if he isn't flat on his back before the end of the first round, he said. Him and Little Owen the Coal have been boxing in the loft over the stables at Gorlan every night since then, to make sure he's really fit. Little Owen the Coal's got a black eye, but no-one can see it cos it's under the coal dust.

You don't say, boy, I said, I thought he looked a bit weird going to work this morning.

Tuesday night came, and the lads had completely filled The Blue Bell yard long before eight o'clock, and a lot of them had to stand by the door and the window cos there was no room inside. But Robin had saved a seat for me cos I was one of the first there, with Huw, and Huw had a seat beside me.

Jesus, it's hot in here, said Huw. You wouldn't think he was a boxer, would you? he said then when Johnny South climbed into the ring through the ropes. And you wouldn't either. His skin was white and he was dancing on his toes in the corner, holding on to the ropes with his back to us.

Yes, but look at his muscles, I said.

They're not a patch on Owen Gorlan's muscles. And look at Owen's skin. It's brown, just like a black man's.

It's sunburned through haymaking.

And there was Owen sitting in his corner facing us and scowling and growling like a mad dog.

Frank Bee Hive was the referee and, after shouting for quiet, he called Owen and Johnny South together and spoke quietly to them for a minute. Then they pretended to shake hands and went back to their corners. Then Roli Pant, who helped Little Owen the Coal at work, hit the big tin lid they were using for a bell and the two of them, Johnny South and Owen Gorlan, jumped to the middle of the ring for the first round.

For the first minute, nobody hit anybody. The two of them just danced about in front of each other with their left arms shooting out as though they were trying to tickle each other's nose. But Johnny South was dancing around Owen, and Owen was watching him like a cat watching a mouse. Then suddenly like lightning, Owen's right arm swung out like a sickle cutting a hedge and his fist caught Johnny South on the side of his ear and he went down on his backside with his legs in the air in the centre of the ring.

One . . . two . . . three . . . Frank Bee Hive shouted into his ear. But before he got to four, Johnny South had jumped to his feet and he was dancing round Owen like before.

Jesus, that was a good punch, said Huw, standing up and then sitting down again all the time, like something gone mad. And by now, everyone was shouting with all their might, especially those at the door and the window.

Another like that for the Southerner, Owen, someone said. But that was the only proper belt that Owen managed to give him. Even though his arms were waving about like a windmill, and shooting straight out sometimes, Johnny South was running rings round him, and wherever Owen Gorlan's fist was, Johnny South's head wasn't.

Then Roli Pant gave the tin lid a bang to say that the first round was over, and the two boxers went back to their corners, neither of them much the worse for wear.

That's science for you, boy, said Huw when the second round started. Owen went at Johnny South like a man cutting hay with a scythe but Johnny South had jumped back. And before Owen had time to get back on the soles of his feet, Johnny South's right hand went straight into the middle of his stomach. Heeerch, said Owen and fell to his knees with his hands on the floor as though he was looking for something. And Frank Bee Hive started counting One, Two, Three but then Roli hit the tin lid to say it was the end of the round.

Owen's skin was shining with sweat as he sat in the corner waiting for the third round, and Little Owen the Coal was hard at it with his towel wiping the sweat off him and whispering to him. But Johnny South didn't look as if he was tired at all. He was standing in his corner, holding the ropes and dancing about just like he was at the start.

Ping, went Roli's tin lid and the two of them jumped out for the third round. Johnny South was a completely different man this time. He looked more serious and was moving more slowly, like a tiger, around Owen, and his eyes were like a dragon's. But Owen was jumping quicker than before with his fists jumping out and waving around Johnny South's head, but without getting a real blow in.

Owen's really mad now, you know, said Huw. Can you see that red patch under his right eye?

Suddenly, Owen's right hand shot out and caught Johnny South right in the face. And the tiger started to back away with Owen really going for him and getting another good punch or two into Johnny's face.

But like lightning, Johnny jumped sideways and his left hand sank deep into Owen's belly, and then his right hand caught Owen on the side of his jaw and Owen started to wobble around like a drunken man with his arms waving in the air.

And we were shouting at the tops of our voices: After him, Owen. Hit him, Owen. And somebody else, who wasn't friends with Owen, shouted: Come on, Johnny South. Lay him out.

And Johnny South did lay him out. Johnny's left arm was the sickle this time, and it caught Owen on the side of his head so hard that his feet left the ground and he landed on the other end of the ring.

One ... two ... three ... said Frank Bee Hive but Owen didn't get up till after he'd said eight. Then he got up very slowly with Johnny watching him like a leopard on the other side, but giving him enough time to pull himself together. Then Johnny South jumped in like lightning and gave Owen another belt with his left hand on the side of his head which lifted Owen off his feet again. But old Owen didn't get up after that one.

One ... two ... three ... said Frank Bee Hive, and after he'd counted ten, he went over to Johnny South and lifted his arm to show that he was the winner, and Johnny was all smiles and showing no sign that he'd been in a fight, and poor Owen was still like a flatfish on the floor, and Little Owen the Coal was throwing water in his face to try and make him come round, and then wiping his face with the towel.

There was a little bit of clapping, but not much, and we all went out before Owen came round, we were so ashamed of him. Some of the big boys went into The Blue Bell and Huw and me and the others went to the Chip Shop next door.

They're good boxers, those Southern lads, said Roli Pant, with his mouth stuffed full of chips and peas.

You wouldn't think he could give Owen Gorlan a hiding with him being only half his size, said Huw.

They teach them while they're little lads, said Roli. You and me would be good boxers if we'd been taught properly when we were little lads. Dew, your chips are good tonight Miss Jones, he said to Ann Jones who was busy putting more fish into the fat.

Afterwards, Huw and me went for a walk up to Stables Bridge to see if Bob Milk Cart or anyone else was trying to catch salmon. But when we got to the bridge, there was nobody there but us two, standing in the moonlight and leaning on the bridge, staring down into the water. And we stayed like that for ages, leaning on the side of the bridge and watching the current and listening to the sound of the water and the wind in the leaves, without saying a word to each other.

Is it us that's going up or is it the River that's going down? I said to Huw at last.

Dew, it's great to get a ride on the bridge for nothing, isn't it? said Huw, laughing.

Have you heard the story about Will Starch Collar, Huw?

Who? That bloke that plays with the Salvation Army Band?

Yes.

No. What story?

The story about him seeing the wheel of fire.

You're joking, boy. I never heard that. Where did he see it?

Right here.

No, boy.

Yes. That's why he went to join the Salvation Army. The

Wheel of Fire came out of the River up this side of the bridge and spoke to him.

No.

Yes, really. And told him to stop getting drunk in The Blue Bell.

Who told him?

The wheel of fire, it's true.

Shut up, you fool. A wheel can't speak.

I know it can't. But there was a Voice in the wheel and it was that that spoke to him.

Who's voice was it?

A spirit voice, of course.

Get away. Who told you?

Mam told me. It was the time of the Revival. Are you scared of spirits, Huw?

Jesus. yes boy.

What would you do if the wheel of fire came up out of the river right here and now?

Nothing. I'd just watch it, to see what'd happen. Look, the moon's in the River down there exactly like a Wheel of Fire. Maybe that's what Will Starch Collar saw when he was drunk.

Yes, but if the wheel of fire rolled up the side of the Bridge to where we're standing and then spoke to you, what would you do?

Jesus, run home as fast as I could.

And then the moon went behind a cloud in the sky and it was pitch black. We'd better go home, said Huw, it's nearly ten o'clock.

Dew, I said, when we reached Post Lane, it'd be great to be able to box like Johnny South, wouldn't it?

Yes, boy.

I wouldn't be scared of anybody, then.

But you're a good fighter, or you wouldn't have been be able to give Johnny Beer Barrel a hiding, that time.

Yes, but that's fighting—not boxing. I'd be scared of lots of things if I couldn't fight. But if I could box properly, I wouldn't be scared of anything ever again.

You'd be scared of ghosts, said Huw laughing, cos you can't box them.

Post Lane was pitch dark, just like it is now, and the moon had gone behind a cloud. And there wasn't a sound coming from anywhere, just the sound of Huw and me in our hobnailed boots, clanking on the Lane.

Jesus, a bogeyman, said Huw suddenly. Look, there it is lying by the side of the Lane there. And we ran for our lives when we heard a voice shout: Go home you little devils.

When we got to the Lockup, Huw stopped running and started laughing his head off.

What's the matter with you, Huw? I said.

But Huw was still laughing. That wasn't a bogeyman, he said at last, it was Little Owen the Coal, drunk.

When we reached the Crossroads, there were a lot of big lads talking to each other. They were talking about Owen Gorlan getting a hiding from Johnny South, but Huw and me didn't stay long to listen.

See you tomorrow, said Huw.

Are you coming with me after school? I said.

Where to?

To ask Johnny South if we can learn to box.

You bet, said Huw. Good night.

Good night.

Where've you been so late? said Mam when I got home. With that old Huw making mischief, I'll bet.

No, really Mam. We went for a walk to Stables Bridge, watching salmon leaping in the moonlight.

You'll grow up a poacher, you know, if you go wandering to that old river like this every night.

We didn't see one poacher there.

No, of course not. The old devils are too sly for anyone to see them.

But d'you know what, Mam? I said after getting a bowl of milky potatoes. The moon was exactly like that wheel of fire you were talking about.

What wheel of fire?

That one Will Starch Collar saw ages ago. Maybe it was the moon he saw, Mam.

Go to bed so I can get on with this ironing.

And maybe it was the man in the moon that spoke to him.

Go to bed, Mam said then, really sharply.

The moon had come out from behind the clouds when I saw it next, after getting undressed and lying in bed and looking out of the skylight. And the old man in the moon was laughing at me and the moon looked exactly like Will Ellis Porter's face.

Then I shouted to Mam from the loft. Mam, I said, could Daddy box when he was a little boy?

There was no answer for a long time, just the noise of the iron going up and down on the table.

Go to sleep, you little villain, said Mam eventually, and stop asking silly questions.

And I went to sleep without asking her anything else.

8

Is this the Voice, I wonder? Or is it just the wind blowing through Adwy'r Nant?

*

I am the Queen of Snowdon, the Bride of the Beautiful One. I lie upon the bed of my ascension, eternally expectant, forever great with child and awaiting the hour of his delivery.

My thighs embrace the swirling mists and my breasts caress the low-lying clouds; they in their precocity explore the secret places of my nakedness, luxuriate amid the wonders of the deep, then rise again in guilty satisfaction to the Heavens.

Thou hast enslaved me. Thou hast enslaved me, my Beloved; and I submit myself unto thy will; with my every living breath do I desire thee.

I would raise my arms in supplication to the Heavens to implore thee my Beautiful One; were it not their fate to be confined to the earth and to remain creations of the clay.

I would lift up my hands begging to the firmament to pray for his munificence; but it is ordained that they should clutch only the dew about my resting place.

I would awake, if my Beloved willed it, to dazzle him with the lustful radiance of my eyes; but my eyelids must not rise from their relentless sleep to gaze upon his glory or to drink in the magnificence of his form.

I would walk to meet him upon the steps of the wind; but feet do not stir which have inherited the shackles of the rock.

The hurricanes roar above my paralysis, and the rain saturates without cleansing; but is there not mercy in the sun, nor pity in the spring breezes?

They amuse me with their petty vows, their empty promises grate upon my ears; the odour of their feeble begging fills my nostrils.

She, the moon of my night-day disturbs my sleep with her shrill laughter; and, in the jealousy of her impotence, shines her fury upon the fruitfulness of my womb.

Come again, my Beautiful One, come again and take me, before the sun rises from his resting place, before we are disturbed by the bleating of the lamb; fully possess your chosen one before the withering of the moon's candle; prepare before me the joy of my afternoon.

And I shall again offer thee my sacrifice; and my sweet incense shall ascend to thy abode.

*   *   *

The early light breathes o'er the darkness of my eyes and I am filled with bliss; for in the afternoon shall come my firstborn.

My arms shall not embrace him neither shall my feet instruct him in his early promenades; yet my breasts shall nourish him and his kiss shall be warm upon my cheek.

I shall show to him the freedom of the high and low expanses; and shall make him expert in the captive methods of the earth.

I shall plant my longing in his bowels; and shall build towers of hope within the city of his skull.

I shall fill the corners of his eyes from the secret wells of my tears; and shall take from the sun and moon his share of laughter.

His form shall be fairer than the unseen day; stronger than the whirlwind shall be the strength of his loins.

I shall push his young one from my womb as a conqueror and demand that he proceed to conquer the world.

The virtue of my breasts shall be for him a light upon his

pathway; the wisdom of my clay shall guide him to the ends of the earth.

Kings and princes shall bow in his presence; and the multitudes shall raise their voices in his praise.

Lands and kingdoms shall be his by right; and great will be the pleasure in his palaces.

His enemies shall grovel for his mercy; pure white virgins shall beg for his lips.

His name shall flit from mouth to mouth; his deeds shall radiate from the writings of the bards.

I shall rejoice in his conquests; I shall call upon the low clouds to celebrate his feast.

*　　*　　*

The afternoon has come; and the spring breezes send their tender waves to caress my blessed burden.

They whisper their tiny dreams into my ears and nostrils; but they bear no tidings of my firstborn.

The sun plaits its silence around the ropes of my hair; its sweat weeps silently upon my brow.

But again the pain of childbirth does not come to make me happy; no pangs of relief gladden my bowels.

I thirst. But I thirst only for the repentance of the rain shower.

The earth rejoices; but the hour of my own rejoicing is not yet at hand.

The lambs leap upon the slope of my shame; bleating and begging for their birthright.

Their music amuses the foothills of the low clouds; but it stirs not, neither does it shear the lamb of my happiness.

How long? How long till my appointed time? How long shall the firmament divert from me the verdure of its mercy?

How long shall the mountains shake their heads; and the hills laugh their scorn upon the childless?

How long shall I wander upon the barren plains of my womb; and the horizon hide the palmtree of my promise?

In vain shall I call upon my comforter; deaf is the earth and deaf are its gods. And dumb are the love-messengers of the Beautiful One.

I lie upon the bed of my humiliation; and beg to be alone in the solitude of the night.

*   *   *

Night's watchfulness is long; and my solitude escapes not the fury of the moon.

Her laughter beats upon my blind eyelids; her scorn penetrates the depths of my captivity.

But hope shall not die; for the sun is not deflected and nought delays the warm progress of the dawn.

But does the Beautiful One not return like a thief in the night to console me? Do I not hear the measured sound of his walking on the floor of the valley?

He shall come, he shall come; and the moon shall hide her jealousy behind the low clouds.

And when he doth return, I shall receive him with the firm breasts of my virginity; I shall know his lips though he comes in the guise of my lost firstborn.

His Wife shall be to him a Mother; and the son shall take unto himself his birthright.

The fires of the moon shall retreat from my heavy eyelids; darkness shall lie upon darkness; and from this night of my confinement to my solitude shall come light.

*

9

After Owen Gorlan got that hiding from Johnny South, everyone started calling him Owen Granny. And this is how he got the name. When he was lying flat on his back after getting that belt from Johnny, and Frank Bee Hive was counting (in Welsh, of course), there was no sign of Owen moving, but after counting eight, Frank Bee Hive suddenly changed to English for some reason. Nine, he shouted (which, when you say it, sounds exactly like nain, the Welsh word for Grandmother) and Owen looked as if he was going to wake up and half-turned onto his stomach. But before Frank could say ten, he collapsed in a heap, flat on his back again, and some comedian pretended he hadn't realised that Frank had changed to English when he said nine and shouted out It's no good, his Granny's not here, Frank, and everyone fell about laughing, even Owen's friends who'd been shown up because he'd had a good hiding.

Owen hasn't got a Granny, you know, said Roli Pant in the Chip Shop.

He was an old Granny, anyway, letting Johnny South give him a belting like that, said one of the other boys.

They'll call him Owen Granny now, you'll see, Huw said to me.

And Owen Granny it was.

But if you'd known my Gran, from Pen Bryn, all those years ago, you would have called me Granny's Baby too.

Gran was a good sort. Every time I get hungry, I think of Gran. Dew, I could do with a really good meal now, too. But it wasn't that that made me think about her now, though. I remember her passing me right here on Post Lane ages ago. How are you tonight? she said to me as though I was a stranger and she'd never seen me before. Bitter weather, eh? she said, although it was as fine as it is tonight. She'd become confused, of course, with her being over ninety at the time.

And when Gran was confused, she used to sneak out of the house without anyone seeing her, and make for Orchard Cottage over there, on the right of Post Lane, where she was born. Nobody lives there now and there are big holes in the roof that you can see the sky through. But in the days when Gran used to go there when she got confused, there were people living there. They were nice people too. And one of them would open the door when Gran knocked and say to her: Come in Betsan Parry. And give her a cup of tea. Then after a little chat, Gran would nip smartly home again and Orchard Cottage would have a break from her for about a month or two, until she started to get confused again.

Gran was a tough 'un, as well. It was her that came to look after us when Mam took ill. Talk about being frightened. Seeing Moi spitting blood was nothing to the fright I got that day when I came home from school and saw Mam sitting in the rocking chair, ill.

It was the middle of winter, and it had been snowing all night. In the morning before going to school, I'd been busy making a pathway through the snow from the door of our house to the middle of the lane and then helping Ellis Evans Next Door and the others to make a pathway down the Hill before they went to work in the Quarry. The snow was reaching higher than the front room window and I thought we'd been buried alive when I woke up. After we'd cut a path down the Hill, there were two high walls of snow on each side and neither Ellis Evans nor Humphrey Top House could see over them, never mind me.

By schooltime, the Hill was like a sheet of glass between the two big walls of snow. Watch you don't fall going down the hill, chick, said Mam.

I won't, I said as I went out through the door. But before I got to the middle of the lane, there I was with my legs in the air and my head on the ground. I felt like some young animal who was trying to walk for the first time. Luckily, Mam had shut the door and didn't see me come a cropper.

After that, I got down into a crouch. I'd learned how to slide down the Hill ages ago when it had frozen before. We only had to stand in the middle of the Hill, and push a bit, very slowly, and then crouch down and we'd be going down the Hill like the Little Train in the Quarry. And there was no need to brake cos the Hill went down to Graveyard Lane, and that was flat, and we didn't stop on the ice until we were at the Graveyard Gate. Then we only had to go through the Graveyard to Post Lane here and we were at school.

Dew, it was cold in school that day, too. And there's one thing I remember very clearly. Price the School had fallen and broken his arm, and it was in a sling. And what was on my mind all day, and made me shake like a leaf sometimes was Price's hand sticking out of the plaster, just like a dead man's hand, as though it didn't belong to him.

I was glad when the bell went for us to go out to play, so I could get warm. We were playing snowballs, of course, and there was a nasty accident in the school yard that day. Someone threw a snowball with a stone in it and it hit Johnny Beer Barrel and broke a hole in his head, and blood was pouring out of it. But he didn't cry or anything, fair play to him, he just went and put his head under the pump to wash the dirt out, and then got a plaster to put on it from Price the School.

When it got to dinnertime, I was really hungry and there was a lovely smell of lobscouse coming from Little Owen the Coal's house and I wondered what sort of a dinner Mam had made for us.

But when I went through the door, there was no cloth on the table or anything, and the house was just like it was empty, except Mam was sitting in the rocking chair. And when she turned her head to look at me, I nearly had a fit. Her face was white as chalk and her eyes were huge, as though they were about to come out of her head. And she couldn't speak, she could only lick her lips and look at me as though she was in a daze.

What's the matter, Mam? I said, nearly crying. Then I ran as fast as I could to the kitchen to fetch her a drink of water, and when she'd drunk some of that, she got a bit better.

Gran, she said, weakly. Go up to Pen Bryn and fetch Gran.

I went like lightning through the door and ran over the ice to Next Door to tell Grace Evans that Mam was ill. And Grace Evans put her shawl on straight away without saying anything and went out to our house.

I'll go and fetch Gran, I said, and ran as fast as I could up to Pen Bryn.

By the time Gran and me got to the house, Grace Evans had put Mam to bed, and the kettle was boiling on the fire and there was a cloth on the table.

It's that old rheumatism, Betsan Parry, said Grace Evans. We'd better get Doctor Pritchard to her.

Can I go and fetch him? I said.

No, she's nice and comfortable now, said Grace Evans. You'd better come over to our house for dinner, and call in on Doctor Pritchard on your way to School.

And that's how it was. And Gran lived with us for three months till Mam got better.

Dew, Gran was a tough 'un, too. I came home one day after being with Huw in the Sheep Field and I was really hungry.

Can I have another piece of bread and butter, Gran? I said.

Like Little Owen the Coal, when he went to help with the haymaking at Gorlan, and they were having their dinner. And Mrs Williams Gorlan asked Owen, just as she was about to cut a slice of bread for him: Do you want a full slice, Owen love?

Yes please, said Owen, and another one to go with it. And everyone fell about laughing except Mrs Williams. She was scowling at him.

But when I said: Can I have another piece of bread and butter, Gran? after eating four, one after the other, what did Gran do in her temper but throw the whole loaf at me across the table.

There, you greedy little devil. You'd better take the loaf to make sure you get enough.

Dew, Gran was a tough 'un. But she was a kind old thing,

too. Talk about performing miracles. For ages, I didn't believe the stories Bob Milk Cart told us in Sunday School about Jesus performing miracles. Turning water to wine, raising people from the dead and suchlike, and especially that story about him feeding the five thousand with five loaves and two fishes. But after that Tuesday when I went to the Church fellowship meeting with Mam, I didn't doubt one of Bob Milk Cart's Sunday School stories about Jesus performing miracles.

It was before Mam fell ill, a year after Humphrey Top House went back to the sea after falling out with Lisa his wife and swearing he'd never come back to her.

But he's sure to come back, you'll see, Mam said to Lisa when she came to our house to say that Humphrey had left her.

But how am I going to live? Lisa said.

Never mind about him, said Mam. You'll get parish money like me if he doesn't come back.

What? said Lisa. Me live on the parish? Never.

Well, there's better folk than you and me had to go on the parish, you know, Mam said.

But Lisa Top House just turned up her nose and went out in a sulk.

She's a strange one, eh Mam?

Yes, chick. She doesn't know what it's like yet, living on the parish. But that's what she might have to do.

Anyway, it was Tuesday night and I'd come home from school in the afternoon nearly starving, and Mam had made milky potatoes.

We haven't got any bread for you to have bread and butter, she said, and as I lifted up my head from my milky potatoes to look at her, I could see she was nearly crying.

Never mind, Mam. Dew, these milky potatoes are good.

We've no more potatoes, either.

Never mind, Mam. I'll get some tomorrow morning after I fetch the cattle. Robin Gorlan'll dig me up a little sackful on the way home.

But what will we do for bread?

Don't worry, Mam. Do you want me to come with you to the Fellowship tonight?

Yes, you'd better come.

And afterwards, we'll go up to see Gran at Pen Bryn.

Alright then.

And off to the Fellowship we went after I'd had a wash and combed my hair after my tea.

Hughes the Parson was at the Fellowship and there was no Choir on a Tuesday night so I sat in our pew with Mam. There was hardly anyone in Church and it wasn't a bit like it was on a Sunday.

After Hughes the Parson had said lots of prayers, he came to the one I liked best of all. That one where he'd pray for the boys who had joined the army and those who'd become sailors. And in the middle of the prayer, he'd say all the boys names in a row, like this:

Elwyn Davies, Earnest Davies, William Evans, Herbert Francis, Robert Wheldon Griffiths, John Hughes, Arfon Jones, Idwal Jones, Hughie Lewis, Alfred Morris, Ifor Owen, Emrys Price, Robert Pritchard, Heilyn Roberts, Ithel Thomas, David Williams, Edgar Williams, John Williams, Ritchie Williams . . .

And afterwards, everyone would keep their heads bowed quietly for two minutes, and think all sorts of thoughts. You could have heard a pin drop.

He didn't say Elwyn Top Row's name tonight, Mam, I said with my head bowed.

Killed yesterday, said Mam very quietly.

And there I was with my head bowed remembering Elwyn Top Row coming home from France the month before, and Huw and me running to meet him coming up Lôn Newydd.

Jesus, you look a mess, Elwyn, Huw said to him. Where have to been to get that muck on your clothes and shoes?

Where d'you think, you daft little devil, said Elwyn. In the trenches, of course. Up to our knees in mud all day, lad, and all night too, for three weeks without moving.

Dew, and he looked tired. But he was full of fun with us.

Look, he said to Huw. Put this on your face and see how nice it smells.

And he gave Huw the gas mask he was carrying on his chest.

This is how it goes on, said Elwyn, and he put the gas mask on Huw's face, and he looked just like a scarecrow.

But it was only on his face for a second before Huw started struggling to pull it off.

Jesus, I'm choking, he said, and started spitting and blowing his nose like I don't know what, and his eyes were streaming. And there was poor old Elwyn falling about laughing at Huw.

Look, you lazy little devils, he said, and stood by the side of the wall to take off the pack that was on his back. You can carry this up to Top Row for me.

And the two of us went with him all the way to Top Row, taking turns to carry his pack, and his Mam came running out of the house like a madwoman and threw her arms round him shouting Elwyn love, Elwyn love, and she was laughing and crying at the same time.

Poor old Elwyn Top Row.

But I was talking about the miracle that happened to Mam and me at the Fellowship that night. It must have started to happen when we were all saying the Lord's Prayer together after singing The Lord is my Shepherd I shall not want.

Our Fa-a-th-e-r who art in Heaven, said Hughes the Parson on his knees.

Who art in Heaven, we said with our heads bowed.

Hallowed be Thy name . . . 'lowed be Thy name . . . Thy kingdom come . . . 'dom come . . . Thy will be done in earth as it is in Heaven . . . Heaven . . . Give us this day our daily bread . . . bread.

And after saying daily bread, I didn't go any further with the others, I just started thinking. I remembered Mam telling me before we came to Church that we had no bread to make bread and butter with, and so I asked God for some more daily bread cos the parish money wasn't coming till Friday.

How can God give me a loaf of bread? I thought to myself. And

93

I started thinking about potatoes and meat and rice pudding and things like that, and remembering the smell of lobscouse coming from Little Owen the Coal's house. And there I was praying on my own, not listening to what the others were saying.

Our Father, I said, who art in Heaven, give us this day a big plateful of potatoes and roast meat, and a big bowlful of rice pudding, and lots of raisin bread, and all sorts of currant cakes and jam tarts, and lots of cheese, and ham and eggs and mushrooms for breakfast, and a new suit for Whitsun and lots of money to spend . . . for Thine is the kingdom, the power and the glory for ever and ever. Amen.

By this time, Hughes the Parson was saying the Blessing and everyone was getting themselves ready to go out. The Peace of God which surpasseth all understanding, said Hughes the Parson, be with you now and for evermore. Amen.

Amen, we said.

And out we went.

It was a fine moonlit night just like tonight as we walked up to Gran's house at Pen Bryn, and there was a light in the kitchen window when we got there, cos Gran hadn't pulled the blinds down.

Hang on a minute so I can see if she's asleep, I said, running ahead of Mam so I could peep through the window. And there was Gran sitting in the armchair by the fire with her glasses on the end of her nose, almost falling off, and her Great Bible was open on her knees with her hands on it and her two thumbs going round and round each other. I thought she was asleep but when I saw her thumbs going round and round, I knew she was only dozing.

Hello Gran, it's us, I said as I opened the door, and Mam came in right behind me.

Come in and close that door, she said. There's a frost tonight and I wouldn't be surprised if we had a bit of snow tomorrow. I was just going to make a bit of supper. You might as well stay and have a bit with me. I won't be long.

And she put the black tape which was attached to the Great Bible in the place where it had been open then she closed it and put it on the round table. And when Gran had gone into the back to fetch the dishes, I went to the Bible to see what she was reading and this is what I saw when I opened it where the black tape was:

The Lord is my shepherd. I shall not want.

I knew the whole psalm cos I'd learnt it in Sunday School with Bob Milk Cart. But there's a strange thing, I said to myself. Gran must have been sitting here reading it at the same time as we were singing it in the Fellowship Meeting in Church.

Margaret Williams Top Row's boy has been killed, said Mam as Gran was putting the dishes on the table.

Gran didn't say anything. She just gave a little sigh, as she very often did for no real reason, never mind someone getting killed.

Hughes the Parson didn't say his name with all the others in the Fellowship Meeting in Church tonight, I said.

It'll be hard on Margaret, losing him, said Mam.

How old was he? said Gran.

Twenty-two last month, said Mam.

They'll all have gone, and us with them, before this old war's over, said Gran. Come to the table. I've not got a lot to offer you tonight.

Gran had made lobscouse for our supper. I preferred Gran's lobscouse to any lobscouse I ever had but I don't know how she ever made it taste so good cos she only got the odd bone once a week from the Butcher' Shop and it was me who brought it for her, on Saturdays. But Gran had lobscouse all through the week, no matter what night it was.

Dew, this lobscouse is good, Gran, I said.

You eat your fill, lad, she said. And then she turned to Mam and said: I'm really glad you called tonight, because something very strange happened when I went out to Ann Jones's Shop this afternoon.

Something strange is always happening in this place, Mam said. Last night, Humphrey Top House came home from the sea again, after telling Lisa that he'd never come back. What happened to you, then?

Well, when I came back from Ann Jones's Shop with six pennorth of potatoes, what did I see on the doorstep but a great big basket full of all kinds of things, butter and sugar and ham and eggs and cheese and two loaves under a basin.

No.

Yes, honestly.

What did you do with them?

The basket and the things are in the back there.

The Boy in Willy Edwards' Shop has made a mistake, not taking the message to the right house, surely. He'll be back for them tomorrow, you'll see.

That's what I thought, too. But when I went through the basket to see what was in it, I found this.

And Gran went into her apron pocket and pulled out a piece of paper. Look what it says, she said to Mam.

And Mam took the piece of paper and pulled out her glasses and put them on her nose and read aloud:

To Betsan Parry, as an offering of thanks. From a Well-Wisher.

Where do you think it came from? said Gran.

Good Lord, I don't know.

It's not your birthday till next month, Gran, I said. So it's not a birthday present, anyway.

No, it's not a birthday present.

Maybe an angel brought the basket from Heaven, I said, remembering how I'd said the Lord's Prayer in the Fellowship Meeting and asked God for all kinds of things. And come to think of it, most of the things I'd asked for to eat were in the basket.

Perhaps the boy's right, said Mam.

Well, whoever brought them, I'd call him an angel, said Gran. Were you saying that Humphrey Top House has come home from the sea?

Dew, that's who the angel was, I'm sure, Gran. He's a really kind man, Humphrey. He gave Mam ten bob last time he was home, and he gave me a lot of nice presents too.

Humphrey. I wonder? said Mam.

Really fair play to him if it was him. Humphrey always was a nice little lad, said Gran. We'll find out one day, for sure. And if he didn't come as an angel from Heaven, he's sure to go back as one doing things like this.

He must be an angel to be able to live with Lisa, anyway.

Do you remember that bellbox I got off him as a present, Mam? I'm sure it's bells like those that ring in Heaven, and Humphrey Top House never did tell me where he got the box from. Maybe that came from Heaven, too.

This boy's talking more nonsense every day, said Gran.

He talks a lot of sense as well though, said Mam, giving me a great big smile. Don't you, chick?

I try, anyway, I said. Can I help you with the dishes and the washing up, Gran?

No, you leave them to me. I want your Mam to come into the back and see the basket. There's far too much in it for me. You'd better take a bit of it back with you.

And the two of them went off together into the back and left me to finish the lobscouse on my own. And there I was eating the lobscouse and still saying Our Father who art in Heaven to myself and trying to think who the devil brought the basket for Gran if it wasn't Humphrey Top House. And if it was Humphrey Top House, I said, Humphrey must be a real angel, and not like everybody else, and somebody must have cut both his wings off when he was a little angel, before he grew up.

You'd better take them in the basket, said Gran in the back.

And the two of them came back, and Mam was carrying the basket full of all kinds of things to eat.

I can only thank you, very much, said Mam.

Oh, don't mention it. You need them more than me. Close that door behind you. I want to read a little bit more.

And Gran took the Great Bible from the round table and sat down in the armchair. And there she was, with her glasses on her nose and her head in the Bible as we passed the window on our way home.

Dew, it was a fine night too, on the way home, a moonlit

night just like tonight, and the moon was laughing at us as he beamed down.

Do you think it was Humphrey? Mam said when I took the basket off her to carry it up the Hill.

No, it was God. I was asking him for everything that's in this basket when I was praying in the Fellowship Meeting in Church tonight.

Were you really, chick?

Yes, really. And it's God that's answered the prayer.

Yes, God does answer prayers. He's answered me many times.

And when I went to bed, Mam was singing pleasantly:

> God fills every earthly space
> Present is he in every place

And I knelt down by the side of the bed to say Our Father before going to sleep. Our Father which art in Heaven, I said. Thank you for Your potatoes and roast meat, and bread and butter and sugar and cheese and ham and eggs and everything else.

There was a real miracle for you, eh?

10

THIS IS ROBIN DAVID'S Field, the one on the right here that
runs all the way down to the Riverbank. Dew, it's a miracle I'm
alive, too, after what happened that day when the Wanderers
came down from Holyhead to play our Celts in the cup.

That was on a Saturday. In mid-week, we used to go over the
wall and across the field to play on the Riverbank after school.
Little Ivor Top Row nearly drowned one day when we went
there, Huw and Little Ivor and me, to play horses with the reins
that Elwyn, Little Ivor's big brother, had made for us out of all
different colours of wool.

Little Ivor was the horse and Huw was the driver holding the
reins, and he had a stick to beat Little Ivor with, instead of a
proper whip. And I was running behind them as fast as my legs
could carry me across Robin David's Field right here. There were
stepping stones to cross the River at the bottom of the field and
that's where Huw was driving the horse to, and Little Ivor was
galloping like mad across the field.

And Huw was shouting: Gee up, Poll. Fast as you can now
over the stones and across the River.

Poll was the name of Little Owen the Coal's mare. That's
where Huw got the name from.

The River had been flooded by the rain, and you could only
see the tops of the stepping stones. But Huw kept driving Little
Ivor onwards, whipping him like hell.

Over the River now, Poll, said Huw, with me behind him.
And Little Ivor leapt onto the first stone and from there onto
the second stone and from there onto the third. And when he

was jumping onto the fourth, right in the middle of the River, he went flying on his backside and slid straight into the water. The reins were long and Huw was only on the first stone behind Little Ivor and I was still in the field by the Riverbank when Little Ivor fell in. But the reins were weak, too, and they broke as soon Little Ivor slipped.

Jesus, what will we do? said Huw, and he jumped back off the stone onto the Riverbank. Ivor was being carried downstream by the flood, and I was running along the Riverbank to keep up with him.

Huw started shouting Help as loud as he could.

Help, I shouted at the top of my voice. And who did we see jumping across the wall from Post Lane and running like lightning across the field but Elwyn, Little Ivor's big Brother.

Ivor's in the River, said Huw at the top of his voice, still running for all he was worth.

Ivor's in the River, I said, just like he did.

By now, Elwyn had caught us up and was running with us. And without taking off his coat or his shoes or anything he dived straight into the River and swam out into the middle and caught hold of Ivor's hair. And in a flash, he'd brought Ivor back to the Riverbank to where we were standing.

Jesus, it was lucky you came, Elwyn, said Huw.

And there was Little Ivor, lying flat on his back, saying nothing, with his eyes wide open staring up in the air, and Elwyn was wiping his face. And Little Ivor looked as though he was in shock.

Are you alright, lad? Elwyn said to him.

Yes, said Ivor, very quietly.

You two go and get some sticks, Elwyn said to us. Then we'll make a fire and dry our clothes. We can't go home like this with our clothes soaking wet.

Damn, said Elwyn, when we'd gathered the sticks and laid them ready. My matches won't light. They're soaking.

I've got a match, I said.

And within two minutes, we had a real bonfire by the side of the River. And there was Elwyn and Little Ivor jumping about stark naked to keep warm, and Huw and me holding their clothes in front of the fire to dry.

Don't tell anyone, lads, remember now, said Elwyn.

Dew, you should get a medal for saving Ivor like that, I said.

Jesus, you should, definitely, said Huw.

And remember specially not to tell Mam or I'll get a hell of a hiding, said Little Ivor.

Maybe I should give you a hiding for being such a stupid little devil and falling into the River, said Elwyn. But we'd better not tell anyone, lads. The old woman will only worry if she finds out. And I'll only get a row, as well, if one of you opens his mouth.

Dew, you should get a medal, said Huw. That's what I say, anyway.

And me, I said.

Elwyn Top Row did get a medal too, before he was killed by the Germans. But he didn't get it for saving Little Ivor, his brother, when he fell into the River.

He got the DCM.

That day when we ran to meet him coming home from France along Lôn Newydd, nobody knew that Elwyn Top Row had won the DCM. It was the next day when Elwyn was still tired out and asleep in bed that the telegram about the DCM came. It was me that took the telegram to Elwyn's house in Top Row. I was on my way home from School at dinnertime and I always called at the Post Office at dinnertime to see if there was a telegram to take to somebody, cos Mr Roberts the Post gave you sixpence for taking a telegram.

Take this to Top Row, he said to me when I went into the Post Office.

And the next day in School, Price told us there'd be no school on Friday and that we were were all going to have a tea party in Stables Bridge School field because Elwyn Top Row had won the DCM.

Dew, that Friday was a great day. There was a procession along the Street from the end of Lôn Newydd right up to the

Church Gate, and then up to Stables Bridge School. And we were all in our Sunday best standing on the pavement watching it, and everyone had been given a flag to wave as the procession went by.

The Llanbabo Band were at the front. The band had come all the way from Llanbabo because Elwyn's cousin played trombone for them. Behind the band was Robin David's coach and horse, and Robin David was sitting up front in the high seat, driving, with a long whip just like a fishing rod.

The top of the coach was pulled down so that everyone could see inside, and there was Elwyn Top Row sitting in the coach just like a Lord, waving and bowing to us, and smiling from ear to ear. And Mrs Williams Top Row, his mother, was sitting beside him in her best clothes, and looking like a Queen at Coronation time. And Little Ivor and his dad were sitting opposite, looking very important and not smiling at all.

Watch you don't fall, Little Ivor, said Huw at the top of his voice as everyone clapped as the coach went by. And everyone was waving their flags. But Little Ivor didn't hear him. And he didn't see us either, because there were too many people on each side of the Street looking at them. And Little Will Policeman's Dad and Jones the New Policeman were marching with the coach, one on each side of it.

Behind the coach were the Oddfellows, marching two by two, and every one of them had a long blue sash across his shoulders and around his stomach. Will Starch Collar was there, and David Evans Snowdon View, and Ellis Evans Next Door, and Humphrey Top House and Bleddyn Evans Garth, and lots and lots of important people, because nobody was working in the Quarry that day.

Come on, said Huw when the Llanbabo Band started playing by the Sixpenny Ha'penny Shop.

And instead of staying where we were, waving our flags, we ran up past the coach and started marching alongside the band. And we marched with it all the way to Stables Bridge School, where the coach stopped and everyone went into the meeting where they gave the medal to Elwyn.

Come on, Huw said after the meeting, or we'll miss the tea party.

And in we went to Stables Bridge School field and started scoffing all sorts of cakes and sandwiches with the others. And afterwards, there was a procession back from Stables Bridge School, with Elwyn and his mam and dad and Little Ivor in the coach just like before, except that Elwyn was wearing his medal on his chest. And the Llanbabo Band were still playing. And we went along with them and marched all the way down to the end of Lôn Newydd.

Dew, that was a great day.

The circus came to Robin David's field as well, and the Lion Show. Hey, it was a miracle that Little Owen the Coal was still alive, too, after that time with the elephant. Little Owen the Coal always was a cruel old devil, even when he hadn't had a drink. We saw him beating Poll the Mare once on Allt Bryn until she nearly collapsed between the shafts. And we were so mad at him that we wanted to stone him to death. But we were too scared of him.

We were standing watching the elephant behind the railings in the Lion Show at the time. A whole row of us laughing at the elephant putting his trunk out through the railings to get nuts and pieces of apple and that sort of thing from us and stuffing them into his mouth.

Watch this, lads, said Little Owen the Coal, and went into his pocket and pulled out a box of matches. And when the elephant put his trunk out through the railings near Little Owen the Coal, he gave him the box of matches. And the elephant put them into his mouth as though they were a nut or an apple, and when he put them into his mouth with his trunk, we saw lots of smoke coming from his mouth. It mustn't have burnt, because he didn't go mad or anything, he just looked with his little eyes at Owen the Coal. And we were all hoping that he'd grab Owen round the waist with his trunk and drag him over the railings and sling him into oblivion.

In fairness to Moi, it wasn't like that with him and the

monkeys. Huw and Moi and me had been let in for nothing for carrying the lions' water for the Show man in the morning. That was a year before Moi died.

How can we get into the Show tonight? said Huw.

Over the wall when nobody's looking, of course, said Moi.

There's no need to go over the wall, I said. The Show man said we can bring the water from the River for him and go in for nothing.

Moi had been to Doctor Pritchard's on the way from School in the afternoon to fetch some medicine for his mam and a box of pills for his Uncle Owen. But we went to the Show before going home. And when we went to see the monkeys, we didn't have any nuts or anything to give them.

Let's see if they like these, said Moi, and went into his pocket for the pillbox.

He threw one in and one of the monkeys snatched the pill and put it in his mouth with his hands. And there was the monkey chewing the pill and staring at us and looking as pleased as Punch.

He likes them, said Moi, and threw another pill in. And one of the other monkeys grabbed it and started chewing it like the other one.

After that, Moi started throwing one pill after another to the monkeys, until he had none left and the box was empty.

Jesus, what will I do now? he said. What will Uncle Owen say when I get home?

Say you've lost them, said Huw.

Or say you didn't get them, I said.

When the people went to the Show that night, there was no sign of the monkeys. And the Show man stood up and told the people that they wouldn't be able to see the monkeys because they'd all been taken ill.

Jesus, I got a hiding from Uncle Owen last night, Moi told us in School the next morning.

What for? Because you'd lost the pill box? said Huw

Or for saying you didn't get them from Doctor Pritchard? I said.

Yes, said Moi. Uncle Owen had seen Doctor Pritchard in the street, and he told him that he'd given them to me. And do you know what they were, lads?

No, said Huw.

Nor me, neither.

They were laxative pills. He's been constipated for three days.

But I wanted to talk about that day the Wanderers came from Holyhead to play in the Cup against our Celts in Robin David's field. It had been raining all day on the Friday and on that Saturday morning, but it had turned fine in the afternoon before the game started.

We were sitting on a wall on the opposite side to Post Lane watching people go into the field, Huw and Moi and me. And there they were in one long line almost down to the Church Gate, going in very slowly, one after the other, after paying sixpence at the gate. Little lads like us could get in for threepence. Little Will Policeman's Dad and Jones the New Policeman were standing by the gate watching the people go in.

Dew, it's bound to be a good game, said Huw. I'd like to see Will Cae Terfyn run rings around the Wanderers' boys. But I've only got threepence and I want to buy sweets for tomorrow and get some chips from Ann Jones' shop on my way home tonight.

I've got threepence too, said Moi. We'll go over the wall after the people have gone in.

I've only got a penny, I said. If I'd gone with Mam to do the shopping instead of coming here, I'd have enough money to pay for all of us.

And there we were thinking how we could get in for nothing when I looked across the road at the gate, where Little Will Policeman's Dad and Jones the New Policeman were standing.

Look, lads, Jones the New Policeman's watching us.

Down off that wall, said the policeman. And we jumped down at once.

Up to Post Lane, said Huw.

Yes, the far end of the field is the best place to go over the wall, said Moi.

I want to stay here for a while to watch the people going in, I said. I'll come after you in two minutes.

And there I was standing with my hands in my pockets, one hand playing with the penny I had, when someone in the row of people who were waiting to be let in waved his hand and shouted to me. I looked behind me, thinking he was waving and calling to someone else, but there was nobody behind me.

Hey, come here, said the man who was waving his hand, and I walked towards him. And who was it but Bleddyn Evans Garth, Ellis Evans Next Door's cousin, who sometimes came up the Hill to visit Ellis and Grace, and came into our house for a cup of tea when there was nobody in Next Door. He worked in the Quarry.

You're the boy from Next Door to Ellis Evans', aren't you? he said.

Yes.

Are you going to watch the Celts win the Cup?

No, I don't think so.

Course you are. Here, take this. Come in with me. And he reached into his pocket and put threepence in my hand.

Lor. Thanks very much, I said.

How's your Mam?

Alright, thanks. I was supposed to go shopping with her this afternoon. But I wanted to watch all the people going into the field. That's why I came here with Huw and Moi.

Oh, so where have they gone?

Up Post Lane for a walk.

Do they want to go in?

Yes, I think so.

Who do you think will win today?

The Celts, of course.

You should wear a green ribbon like me to show what side you're on. Here, I'll cut this in two so you can have half.

Lor, thanks a lot.

And Bleddyn Evans took the green ribbon from his chest and

106

went into his pocket for a knife and cut it in two and gave half to me.

Have you got a pin?

No.

Here you are, take this.

Lor, thanks again.

I looked a proper swell going through the gate into the field with Bleddyn Evans Garth, with the green ribbon on my chest. And when the Celts boys came onto the field, I was shouting C'mon the Celts louder than anybody.

I fancy going over there to find a better place to see, I said to Bleddyn Evans.

Yes, you go if you like. I'm fine right here.

And I walked very slowly up the line to look for a gap between the men who were standing along it, so I could find a good place to watch, and shout C'mon the Celts.

God, look who's here, said someone, when I'd walked almost right up to the Celts' goal line. And who should be there but Huw and Moi, looking as guilty as two dogs who'd been killing sheep.

How the devil did you get into the field? You said you only had a penny, said Moi.

Hey, how did you two get in, then?

Over the wall over there of course, while Little Will Policeman's Dad and Jones the New Policeman were at the other end.

Hey, you look great with that green ribbon, said Huw.

I got it from Bleddyn Evans Garth, Ellis Evans Next Door's cousin. He cut the one he had in half with a knife and gave half to me.

Yes, but how did you get into the field?

Bleddyn Evans gave me threepence so I could come in with him. He's down in the bottom end over there. I came up here so I could see better.

C'mon the Celts, said Huw at the top of his voice as the ball came up to the Celts' goalmouth and Will Roberts the Goalie leapt for it and kicked it out into midfield.

Look, I said, you'd both better have a bit of this green ribbon to show which side you're on.

And I took the ribbon off and cut it in three pieces and gave one to each of them and kept one for myself.

Have you got a pin? said Huw.

Here you are, said Moi. Everyone will think we've paid to get in now.

We can go round to that side, by the River, said Moi. There's less people and more room over there, and Jones the New Policeman's coming up.

Dew, that Will Cae Terfyn's a good dribbler, said Huw when we'd found a space halfway up the touchline on the River side of the field.

And you should have seen Will Cae Terfyn running rings round the Wanderers' boys, too. Whenever he got a pass from the left wing or the right wing, Will was running down the field with the ball as though it was attached to his feet by a piece of elastic. Then, when he was coming up to one of the Wanderers' boys, he'd stop dead and the ball would stop in front of him. Then he'd do a little dance on each side of the ball with the Wanderers' lad watching him like a cat watching a mouse. And before he knew where he was, Will Cae Terfyn had tapped the ball through his legs with the front of his foot and run round him, and left the Wanderers' boy on his backside in the mud. Then Will was going straight through the others like a knife through butter until he was at the Wanderers' goal.

They say that Everton and Aston Villa have tried to get Will Cae Terfyn, said Huw as Will was weaving his way towards the Wanderers' goal.

They won't get him, you know, said Moi. He'd rather stay with the Celts.

Goal! the three of us screamed at the top of our voices as Will scored the first goal. Will had shot the ball into the net, and there was the Wanderers' goalkeeper on his belly in the mud, with his feet in the air and his arms out as though he was trying to reach all the way to Post Lane. And all the people on the line were shouting and dancing like lunatics, and all the Celts' boys were running up to Will and shaking his hand and putting their arms round him and tussling his hair. And the referee had his whistle in his mouth and was running back to midfield.

That Titch is a good referee, said Moi.

We called him Titch because he was a tiny little man, and he had a mop of curly black hair. And when he was running backwards and forwards between the lads, and bending down to watch the ball, with his whistle in his mouth, he looked smaller than Little Bob Pen Clawdd, the one we always made fun of because he was only as tall as he was wide and he was forty. And when Titch was standing up, he barely came up to the knees of Will Roberts, the Celts' goalkeeper. Dew, he was a tall one.

Ritchie Hughes Pen Garnedd scored the second for the Celts, just before the end of the first half. Ritchie and his two brothers, Albert and Llywelyn, played for the Celts' team. Dew, they were three good players, too. But Ritchie was the best of the three. He had a kick like a mule in his left foot, and that goal Ritchie scored was the best one I ever saw. He was running alone with the ball down the Celts' left wing, just where we were standing and shouting C'mon the Celts. And when he'd just crossed the centre line and was zooming past us, he took a shot. The ball flew through the air and was heading for the far corner of the Wanderers' goal, just under the crossbar, and the Wanderers' goalkeeper was leaping from the other post with his arms stretched out trying to save it.

It went over, said Moi.

Did it hell, goal, said Huw.

Goal, I said at the top of my voice, and Titch blew his whistle and then everyone shouted Goal at the top of their voice. And then Titch gave a long blow on his whistle to say it was half-time.

The cup's ours, said Huw, when we'd walked to the Riverbank and were throwing stones into the River to kill time.

Don't be too sure, said Moi. The field's all muddy and the Celts' lads are tired. And they'll be playing against the wind now, with the sun in their eyes as well.

Then Titch blew his whistle, and we walked back to the line.

Foul, said Moi at the top of his voice, as soon as the game had restarted. There's a dirty devil for you.

One of the Wanderers' boys had tackled Will Cae Terfyn from behind and made him slide on his belly through the mud for about four yards. And Titch didn't take any notice or blow his whistle or anything. He just waved his hand to tell the lads to carry on playing. But the people round the field were screaming like lunatics, and lots of them were swearing and cursing and calling Titch all kinds of names. And Bleddyn Evans and a gang of others with him were having a blazing row on the line with Jones the New Policeman.

And while all this was going on, a little voice from somewhere shouted: Goal! And as we looked, there was the ball in the Celts' goal and Will Roberts was flat out in the mud. Everyone was quiet for a long time after that.

Two one, said Huw. Jesus, I hope they don't get another goal.

But between the mud and the tackling and the pushing, the game got dirtier and dirtier, and Titch was always blowing his whistle for a foul. And it was hard to tell who were the Celts in their red shirts and who were the Wanderers in their yellow shirts because the lads were covered in mud from head to foot, and you couldn't see their colours. And the Wanderers' lads were forever pressing forward and the ball was always in the Celts' goal area, and Will Roberts was under terrible pressure and fisting the ball away all the time with his arms going round like a windmill. And the Wanderers' goalkeeper wasn't doing anything except walking backwards and forwards and rubbing his hands and his legs to keep warm cos he had nothing else to do.

Will Roberts had punched the ball away three times with both fists together and everyone was shouting Great stuff, Will and C'mon the Celts. And suddenly, Titch blew his whistle and someone shouted Goal! And there was the ball sitting in the mud on the Celts' goal line and all the lads were round Titch arguing like hell. But the referee was stooping forward with his whistle in his mouth and running for the centre line with the lads running after him, still arguing, and the people on the touchline were screaming like lunatics.

It didn't go in, lads, said Huw.

I don't think so either.

Nor me neither.

But the maddest one of all was Will Roberts the Goalie. There he was, with his face all red, walking up and down and punching the air, and showing the ball in the mud on the goal line to the people around him.

Suddenly, Will Roberts sat down in the mud by the post and put his head in his hands as though he wanted to cry. Then he got up and started galloping like mad towards midfield, where the other lads were still arguing with the referee.

And before anyone knew what was happening, Will Roberts had got hold of Titch by the scruff of the neck with both hands and lifted him off his feet and turned round and was carrying him like that back to the Celts' goal, and Titch's feet were kicking the air underneath him, as though he was riding a bike.

When Will Roberts and Titch reached the goal, Will put him down and pointed to the ball in the mud on the line and started arguing with him again. But Titch was still arguing back. So Will grabbed him and pushed his head down until his nose was in the mud next to the ball.

Will you believe it now then, you stupid old bugger? Will said to him.

Everything went completely to pot after that.

A lot of people who were on the touchline ran into midfield and started arguing with the Wanderers' lads, and some of them were running towards the Celts' goal to try to get hold of Titch and murder him. But Little Will Policeman's Dad and Jones the New Policeman were there before them and had put Titch between them and were telling people to keep away. But I'd never seen people so completely wild with anger.

Then Little Will Policeman's Dad called the lads from the Celts and the Wanderers together and, after talking for a little while, they made a ring around the referee and started to walk off the field with the people walking on all sides of them shouting, and some of them cursing and swearing.

Talk about Elwyn Top Row's procession. The one with Titch was the most fantastic procession I ever saw in my life.

Then as we were walking down past the Church Gate, with Titch in the lead, and the two policemen one each side of him, and the lads from the Celts and Wanderers behind them, and the people behind them shouting and throwing clumps of grass and mud trying to hit Titch, Moi said: I'm going to get a clump of turf.

No, leave him alone, said Huw.

But Moi went off to look for a clump of turf. And the next thing we saw was this enormous clump of muddy turf flying through the air. But instead of hitting Titch, it landed smack on Little Will Policeman's Dad's ear and knocked his helmet off. But Little Will Policeman's Dad did nothing except bend down and pick up his helmet and put it back on his head and carry on walking until they were at The Blue Bell, where the lads always got washed and changed. And in they went with Titch. And a lot of the people were standing around The Blue Bell arguing for ages. But nobody saw Titch come out, because they took him out of the back door.

Was it you that threw that clump of mud that hit Little Will Policeman's Dad? said Huw on the way home.

No, definitely not, said Moi. I couldn't find a clump. Some people are saying it was Little Will Policeman that threw it.

Jesus, he'll get a hiding when he goes home, if it was him, said Huw.

Dew, that was a terrible day. There's no-one playing football on Robin David's Field now. Only cattle grazing.

I I

WHO WALKS AMONG the garden's flowers by dawning's early
light; None crucified by hand of man more beauteous in our
sight . . .

And then the voices rose until they could be heard in the
furthest part of the valley

> Jesus it is He-ee
> Jesus it is He-ee
> Jesus it is He-ee . . .

And then going very quiet as they sang the last line:

> That di-i-i-i-ed u-p-o-n the Tr-ee-ee

It was over there on the side of the Braich that they were
standing together, that Choir that came here from the South to
raise money cos the coal mines had gone on strike. And we'd
come up from Church after the service to listen to them, and
chapel folk had come too, and all the people who were walking
up and down Post Lane had stopped to listen.

It was the year after the War ended and, on the Wednesday
before, they'd been unveiling the Memorial by the Church Gate.
We'd been one of the first to get a Memorial and they'd chosen
Wednesday to unveil it because all the shops in the street closed
on Wednesday afternoon.

Dew, that was a strange day too. Everybody was dressed in
black and it was as though fifty funerals were going on at once,

cos there were fifty lads' names on the Memorial, and all the names shone like gold on the stone when they unveiled it.

It was John Morris Gravestones who made it. Dew, John Morris was good at drawing pictures and carving names on gravestones. He could make angels too, and they stood on top of the gravestone with wings, just as though they were alive and about to fly out of the graveyard. But carving names and Bible verses and pictures on slate was what John Morris did best.

What do you think of this, lads? he said to Huw and Moi and me one day when we went to the yard to see what kind of gravestone he was making for Griffith Evans Braich after he got killed in the Quarry.

Dew, it's a nice one, isn't it? said Huw.

And this is what was on the stone. A picture of two hands, holding each other and shaking hands. And underneath them

IN LOVING MEMORY
of
GRUFFYDD EVANS
12 ERYRI TERRACE, BRAICH

who died September 24, 1915
aged 55 years

In the midst of life we are in death

You haven't spelt his name right, said Moi. Griffith Evans was his name.

No, my boy, said John Morris. I never spell anyone's name wrong. Everyone called him Griffith Evans, you know, but Gruffydd Evans was his real name.

Uncle Owen used to call him Griff Braich, said Moi.

Yes, your Uncle Owen and he were great friends.

Is that a Bible verse at the bottom? I said.

Yes, it comes from the Bible, said John Morris.

But anyway, the Memorial was the greatest piece of work John Morris ever did, and he was there at the unveiling in his Sunday best and he had a seat at the front with all the important people.

They sang Lead Kindly Light first. Dew, I want to cry every time I sing that:

> Lead kindly light, amid the encircling gloom
>   Lead thou me on
> The night is dark and I am far from home
>   Lead thou me on

And I think about a little light like that one over there just starting to appear between the clouds in Nant Ycha.

Huw and me both had a new suit for the unveiling, and we'd both got long trousers for the first time.

Moi would be in long trousers today if he been allowed to live, said Huw, as we stood behind the people, singing with a hymn book between us. We weren't in the Choir because our voices were starting to break.

He would too, boy, I said.

Everyone was thinking about dead people that day, especially after the sermon Hughes the Parson gave after the unveiling.

This is a sad day in our history, said Hughes the Parson in his sermon. But it is also a day on which we should be proud. A day of sorrow and of joy. Sorrow for the loved ones who have been taken from us; sorrow for the empty homes; sorrow for the children and the grandchildren who have not come home; sorrow in the profound yearning we feel for those who have been taken from us in the full bloom of their youth.

And all the women had their hankies out and were crying quietly, and some of them were saying Our Father as well, loud enough for everyone to hear them. And all the men had their heads bowed and looked sad.

And Huw and me weren't saying anything, we were just thinking about poor Moi in the Graveyard.

And then Hughes the Parson carried on, with the wind blowing his white hair all over his head.

But of pride too, he said. Pride for our sons' sacrifice; for their readiness to offer up their lives on the altar of freedom and to defend their country against violence and oppression.

And not only of pride, said Hughes the Parson, beginning to raise his voice and almost sing his words. Not only of pride, but also of joy. Joy for the victory we have achieved through their sacrifice; joy for the certainty we have through Christ that we shall see them all again in a day yet to come, all robed in white and in new bodies like our Lord coming glorious from the grave.

By this time, most of the women had stopped crying, and everyone was standing up and singing together:

> If I must render back to thee
> The finest gift e'er giv'n to me
> This shall I say and cheerfully
> Thy will be done

And because there were a lot of English people there, we sang Abide With Me to finish the service.

But I was talking about the Choir from the South who were singing on the side of the Braich over there the following Sunday night. Everyone had been having another look at the Memorial and a lot of fresh flowers had been placed around it. And Huw and me had been looking at it too, and reading the cards that were with the flowers when we'd been for a walk up by Stables Bridge and come up to here to hear the Choir from the South.

Aw, poor things, it's a shame for them, you know, said Huw.

They're on strike, aren't they? I said.

Yes. Their wives and children are starving in the South, and they're going round raising money to buy food for them.

Where are they staying?

They haven't got anywhere to stay. They arrived here today and the people in the village are giving them beds. Two of them are coming to stay with us tonight.

Dew, it's a pity we haven't got any room at home. I'm sure Mam would let them come to stay with us.

And the Choir was singing:

116

As we remember the garden, his crying out loud
 And his sweat run like droplets of blood,
A back once so beautiful now cruelly ploughed
 And struck down by His own Father's sword
And His journey to Calvary hi-i-i-ll
 Where though dying, no sorrow he felt
Which tongue can be about this be sti-ill
 Which heart is so hard 'twill not melt

Jesus, they're good singers, said Huw. They're far better than our Temperance Choir. Do you know why?

No, I don't know.

It's the coal dust that gets in their throats. That's what gives them good voices.

Give over, you fool.

It's true. That's what my Dad says anyway.

But Quarry dust gets in the men's throats in the Temperance Choir too. That's what Mam was telling me. That's why some of them drink so much, the old rascals, Mam says.

Yes, but coal dust must be better than Quarry dust for making people good singers.

By this time, more people than ever had come up to join us, and everyone had crowded together around the South Choir, so that Huw and me were stuck in the middle of them. The people who had stopped to listen on Post Lane had come in through the gate, so that the side of the Braich over there was black with people. The whole village was there, very nearly.

Dew, it was a lovely light night too, not a moonlit night like tonight, because it was September then, and the sun hadn't gone down and it was still shining on the little rocks on the side of the Braich. And someone had been making a gorse fire on top of the Braich, and the smell of it was coming towards us, carried on the wind.

In Eden's land shall I recall

then the Choir sang:

117

I blessings countless lost them all
No crown of life I wo-ore
But victory of Calvary-y-y
Won salvation back for me-e
I shall sing forevermo-o-ore

And all the people listened quietly, as though they were in Church or Chapel, until the Choir came to the last verse:

Faith there's the place and there's the Tree
Where Heaven's Prince was nailed for me
Truly took he my blame.
The dragon bruised by God in man
Two lay wounded, one had won
And Jesus was his name.

Suddenly, David Evans and a group of men from the Temperance Choir who were standing with him at the front, close to the South Choir, struck up the song:

The dragon bruised by God in man
Two lay wounded, one had won

And before they came to the last line, the man who was conducting the South Choir, who had his back to us conducting his choir, turned round to face us and raised his arms and started conducting David Evans and the others, who were singing at the top of their voices:

And Jesus was his name.

Then the conductor raised his hand and told us all to sing, and turned to the South Choir to tell them to sing, then turned round to the people, until Huw and me and all the people around us were singing our hearts out, and our voices were being carried on the wind up and down the Valley until people must have been able to hear us from the end of Lôn Newydd to the end of Black Lake, if there was anyone there listening.

118

> The dragon bruised by God in man
> Two lay wounded, one had won
> And Jesus was his name.

Streuth, there was no end to it. And Huw and me were beginning to think that we'd never stop singing, when the conductor put his hand up to tell us to be silent. And when, at last, we were silent, he turned round to his choir and raised his hand to one of the men who was standing on the left-hand side. And he began to sing a solo on his own, and the conductor turned back round to face us, and stood with his arms down listening just like us. Dew, he was a good tenor that chap, as well:

> The One who then was crucified
> For a sinful man like me
> Who drained the cup completely
> Himself on Calvary

When he said Calvary the conductor lifted his arms suddenly to tell us to come in, and everyone began to sing at the top of their voice:

> The source of Everlasting Love
> The peaceful home all minds do crave
> Takes me to that covenant
> Ne'r broke by death nor broke by grave

Things got even worse then, and even when the conductor raised his hand to tell us to be silent, the people didn't stop singing. Huw and me weren't sure whether we were singing or crying. I had a big lump in my throat, anyway, and Huw had put his arm round my shoulders, and I could tell by his voice that he had a big lump in his throat, too. Dew, and ever since then, I get a lump in my throat every time I sing those words:

> . . . peaceful home all minds do crave
> Takes me to that covenant
> Ne'er broke by death nor broke by grave

119

But things got stranger than ever after the people stopped singing. It was as though the silence was pressing in on us until we couldn't stand it anymore. The sun had gone down behind the Braich and it was beginning to get dark. And a cold wind began to blow through the trees all around us and make an eerie sound in the leaves, and it drove a cold shiver through us, as though the place was full of ghosts. And on the other side of Post Lane, on the right over there, the slates were shifting on the old Quarry tip, and making a noise like they are now. But at the time, Huw and me thought it was the voices of the all the people singing that was disturbing them. But, apart from the sound of the wind in the leaves and the noise of the slate shifting on the tip, there wasn't the slightest sound from anyone. The people just stared like young calves at the man conducting the South Choir, and everyone had a strange look on their face as though they were waiting and waiting for something but they didn't know what.

Suddenly we saw David Evans at the front beside the South Choir raising his hand to the people.

Let us all join together in prayer, he said.

And without anyone saying a word to them, everyone fell on their knees on the grass, Huw and me with them, and everyone bowed their heads and closed their eyes. And David Evans' voice was praying. But no-one knew what he was saying because the wind was carrying his voice away. But everyone was praying on their own, because we heard some of them near us mumbling to themselves. We only knew one proper prayer, apart from Our Father, and that was one they'd taught us when Huw and me were confirmed. And that was the one we said then. I still remember it too:

May the fear of your Holiness be upon me, O blessed Lord, to keep me safe in this world. And may your love be the object of my life and a comfort to me in the hour of my death. For thy mercy's sake, Amen.

But it was too short a prayer to last all the time the people were on their knees, and when I'd finished it I had nothing to say to myself. And I couldn't think of anything. I just listened to the sound of the wind in the leaves and the noise of the slates on the Quarry tip and David Evans' voice being carried away on the wind. And when I heard David Evans saying something about dying, I started thinking about Moi in the Graveyard, and about Elwyn Top Row in France, and about Moi's Uncle Owen hanging on a rope, and about Em, Little Owen the Coal's Brother in his coffin on the sofa, and a lot of other people I knew who had died.

Dew, I'd like them to sing In the great waters and the waves, I said to myself. There is none to hold my head. And I thought about Little Ivor being carried down the River flat on his back after the big flood and Elwyn saving him.

But Huw had a weird look about him when I opened my eyes and looked at him. His face was white as chalk and his eyes were closed and he must have been crying quietly, because there were tears on his cheeks like there were on the day of Moi's funeral. And I remembered Moi asking me in School how Price the School could cry with his eyes closed, that day he got the news about Bob Price being killed.

Are you alright, Huw? I said quietly.

Dew, where are we? said Huw, opening his eyes and wiping them with his coat sleeve. Yes, boy, I'm okay.

When David Evans had stopped praying, and when we'd been quiet for a long time afterwards with everybody still on their knees, we saw the conductor of the South Choir stand up and raise his hand to the people.

Let us now sing, he said, talking just like Johnny South. Everyone stay on their knees. And we'll sing, as a tribute to the lads whose names are on your Memorial, a well-known hymn by Evan Glan Geirionydd, Those faithful with blessings deserved. Now then. And he began conducting, and everyone was on their knees, singing.

> Those faithful with blessings deserv-ed
> Who from us, the living, go on,
> Their names be forever preserv-ed,
> Such peace is there now for each one.

> After all their sore grievous affliction
> Lie they now quietly far from the rave,
> Far from noise of this world and its friction
> without pain in the dust of the grave

That's how we were singing, nice and quietly, without anyone getting worked up or anyone singing at the top of his voice, like we were a little while ago. The slates had stopped making a noise on the Quarry tip too, and the wind had stopped making a noise in the leaves. It was as though a lot of friendly ghosts had come out of the woods and were walking through the people and putting their hands on everyone's forehead and soothing them. But if those ghosts did come, they must have walked straight past some of the people without putting a hand on their foreheads, because there were a few raising their voices a bit afterwards as they sang the last verse:

> Come no more voice of the tyrant
> To wake them to weeping again,
> No cross nor no cruel tribulation
> For they shall no longer know pain.

It was just about dark by this time, and everybody stood up and started chatting to each other. And two of the South Choir went round with their caps to collect money.

Do you want to give something, Huw? I said. I've got tuppence. I'm going to give a penny.

Me too. Do you see that one who's coming this way? He's one of the two who are coming to stay with us.

How are you, young 'un? the man said, beaming at Huw.

Fine thanks, said Huw, and put a penny in his cap.

And I did the same.

Dew, I feel ill, boy, said Huw when he'd gone. I want to throw up. Lets go home through Lôn Goed instead of along Post Lane.

Alright then.

And when we came to the wood, out of sight of the other people, Huw started to throw up.

Ate too much at dinnertime, he said when he'd finished. Dew, I feel better now. That was the best singing I've ever heard, boy. Do you know what I'd like?

No.

To be a parson.

And me too, boy.

And do nothing but sing and pray all day long.

You'd have to stop swearing.

Dew, I'll never swear again.

And stop smoking.

But Hughes the Parson smokes.

Yes, but he shouldn't, by rights.

I've stopped swearing. And I'm never going to smoke anymore either.

Me neither.

Do you think they'll laugh at us in school?

I don't care about them. And I'll be going to work in the Quarry next year.

There's a lot of good men working in the quarry. Men like David Evans.

Yes. And like Will Starch Collar.

Yes. But he's a real Godly man. He was converted.

We might have been converted too, you know. But I don't want to be Godly. I just want to be good.

And me too.

And there we were making all kinds of resolutions, until we came out of the wood at the end of Lôn Newydd.

Good night now, said Huw. The two men from the South Choir will have arrived at the house by the time I get home. See you in school tomorrow.

Good night, Huw.

There was no-one on Lôn Pen Bryn on the way home, and everyone must have arrived home from the side of the Braich because there were lights in the windows of the houses on both sides of the lane. I could still hear the voices of the South Choir and the people singing in my ears, and I was thinking about myself grown up, a parson, and preaching from the pulpit every

123

Sunday, and telling the Church people all kinds of things about God and Jesus and the Holy Spirit. And Huw was the warden in the Church with me, and everybody was saying what a good man he was. Dew, I was feeling fine, and in a great mood, and saying that I wanted to be more good than anyone else. It was exactly as if I'd been converted. And I was hurrying home to tell Mam.

And when I opened the door and went in, I was going to say: I've been converted, Mam. But when I saw her face, the words stuck in my throat. And I stopped in my tracks and just looked at her. She was sitting in the rocking chair and she looked as though she'd been crying. And her face was white as chalk.

I'd seen her like that once before. And that was when she'd got out of bed after being ill for three months, when Gran was with us. When I was going to School that morning, I didn't know that Doctor Pritchard had let her get up. But when I came home from school, there she was, sitting in the rocking chair looking into the fire, and I only saw the side of her head as I came through the door.

And that time too, when I saw her in the chair I was going to say: Hurray, Mam's up. And the words were on the tip of my tongue when she turned her head to look at me. But the words stuck in my throat. Because her face wasn't the same as it was before she was ill. Or even the same as it was when she was lying in bed in her room. Her face was white as chalk, like a face in a coffin, except her eyes were open, and they were shining black like blackcurrants and when she looked at me, they went through me like steel pins. Dew, I was frightened when I saw her that time. But then she laughed at me and I wasn't frightened any more.

But she wasn't laughing that evening when I went home thinking I'd been converted. She'd been crying, and she looked crazy, and her eyes were going through me like steel pins, like the time before.

What is it, Mam? I said, frightened.

Your Uncle Will's been here, she said, still looking at me with her steel pin eyes.

The swine, I'll kill him if he comes here again, I said, losing my temper and forgetting all about being converted.

Uncle Will was Mam's brother. He'd lived with us ages ago, when I was a little baby, and he used to play the organ sometimes in Church in those days, in place of Frank Bee Hive's Dad, till he started getting drunk and got thrown out of the Quarry cos he'd been on a drinking spree. After that, he became a tramp and Mam never mentioned him again and nobody knew anything about him. Until that night he came to our house about a year before the evening of the South Choir.

It was midnight, and Mam and me were in bed, when there was a knock at the door. And Mam got up and went to the door.

Who's there? she said, without opening the door. I was listening, frightened.

Open this bloody door, said a drunken man's voice outside.

Uncle Will, I said to myself, shaking like a leaf.

And I heard Mam shout: Get away. Get away from here. You'll never set foot in this house again.

And Uncle Will was making a noise like a dog growling outside. And then everywhere was quiet. And Mam came back into the room shaking like a leaf. Afterwards, we both went to sleep without saying a word.

Did he come into the house? I said on the evening of the South Choir.

Yes, said Mam, and started crying quietly.

After that, I couldn't get any sense out of her. She didn't take any notice if I spoke to her. She just kept looking through me, and talking to herself, or to someone she thought was standing behind her.

You old devils, she said, looking behind her. Yes, it was you that brought that swine here.

And she just carried on, arguing with someone who wasn't there.

I went to bed, very downhearted.

12

WHY THE DEVIL did I come this way along Post Lane tonight? I could have gone for a walk over the Mountain or over the side of the Foel. I'm sure it would have been nicer going on either of those two roads than it is here on Post Lane.

In the Summer holidays, I used to go with Mam over the Mountain to visit Auntie Ellen at Bwlch Farm. Dew, it was a nice little farm she had, too. Two cows and a calf in the cowshed, and two sows in the pigsty, and lots of hens running around the place, and a field in front of the house with a plum tree in it, full of big black plums. And a swirling lake and a hay barn. It was in the hay barn that I broke my arm.

Mam used to go over the Mountain to see Auntie Ellen every week, but I was only allowed to go with her in the School holidays. And she always went on a Wednesday cos by Wednesday the food would be running out and the parish money didn't come till Friday. She used to take a big net shopping bag with her, and bring it back full to bursting with all kinds of things to eat, things Auntie Ellen had given her to bring home.

Dew, it was a lovely day, as well, when I broke my arm at Bwlch Farm. Mam and me had set off across Stables Bridge first thing in the morning cos it was four hours' walk over the Mountain to Bwlch Farm. And it was only just beginning to get light as we were climbing up through Rhiw Woods and coming up to the Mountain Gate.

It's only just getting light, I said when we stopped to catch our breath by the Mountain Gate.

No. It's been light for over an hour, said Mam. It's all these trees that make it dark.

Is it true that there are bogeymen in Rhiw Woods?

Oh yes. People have seen them.

We didn't see one, though.

Well, it was too dark.

Lor, look, there's County School down there. It looks nice from here, doesn't it, with the sun on it?

Yes, that's where you'll be going if you pass your scholarship.

Dew, yes. And I'm sure to pass.

After walking along the Mountain for about half an hour, Mam pointed to a little old building with broken windows on the side of the mountainside.

Do you see over there? she said. That was the School I used to go to when I was a girl.

Lor, it's small. No-one goes to School there now though, cos all the windows are broken.

No, there's a new school now, on the other side of the Mountain. And do you see that row of houses, in the valley over there?

Yes, I see.

That's where I used to live when I was a little girl. That's where I was born.

No. What did you do when you left School?

I went into service in Manchester.

Lor, I didn't know you'd been as far as that.

Yes. Manchester's a fine place. I'll take you there one day so you can see the Lion Show at Belle Vue.

After we'd walked for about another hour, and gone through the next Mountain Gate, we could see Bwlch Farm ahead of us, a long way off in the distance. There was a narrow track going up the mountainside and by the side of the track, halfway up, was Bwlch Farm.

There's Auntie Ellen, I said. I can see her standing in front of the house in her white apron.

You've got better eyes than me, said Mam. She's feeding the chickens, I expect.

And there's someone in the Big Field too.

That must be Guto, your cousin, picking up stones.

Dew, I was thrilled to bits when Bwlch Farm came into view. I completely forgot that I was tired, and thought about the proper dinner we'd get from Auntie Ellen and the fun I'd have with Guto.

Hello Gel, I said when we'd gone up the Hill and turned into the little track that led to Bwlch Farm. Auntie Ellen's dog was really called Gelert but everyone called him Gel. And Gel started jumping all over us and barking like mad. He was a great one for giving you a welcome, old Gel.

You go to the Big Field and help Guto collect stones, said Mam as soon as we'd gone into the house and sat down.

Let the little lad sit down for a minute, so he can have a cup of tea and get his strength back, said Auntie Ellen.

Auntie Ellen was a nice woman, but I never saw her laugh. Even when she was talking happily, she had a sad look about her. And her mouth always looked as though she was complaining about something. And Catrin, my cousin, Guto's little sister, was sitting in the corner as usual, not speaking to anybody. Catrin had burned her face when she was a little girl when a kettle fell off the fire and scalded her, and her face looked terrible with the skin all shiny and pink and wrinkled. She never went out or said how are you to anyone even though she was nearly fifteen. She just sat by the fire all day reading or knitting stockings.

Can I go to the Big Field to help Guto now? I said when I'd had a cup of tea and got my strength back.

Yes, you go now. said Mam, and don't get into mischief.

Guto was a big strong lad, with jet black hair and a thin white face, and dark eyes, and a bit of red on his cheeks just like Moi used to have. But Guto didn't have TB cos he passed the test to go into the army the next year, and he didn't get killed by the Germans until the last day of the War. But Auntie Ellen and Catrin were dead by then, and he would have been all on his own at Bwlch Farm if he'd come back.

Whenever Guto came to visit us, he'd be wearing knee-breeches with shiny brown leggings. But when I went to join him in the Big Field, there he was with a wheelbarrow picking up the stones in his long trousers that he'd made short by tying two pieces of string round his knees, just like the Quarrymen.

How goes it, Guto? I said.

Hello, lad. I see you've come at last, and here's me almost finished collecting the stones. If you go over there, we'll be finished in less than half and hour.

Can I take the wheelbarrow, Guto?

Sure, if you can roll it.

Course I can. Dew, it's heavy.

The barrow was almost full of stones and when I tried to lift it, it fell over on its side.

You careless little devil, said Guto, coming to turn the barrow straight again.

Dew, it was heavy.

You'd better eat more bread and milk to make your muscles grow. Lift all the stones back into the barrow, now.

And there I was lifting the stones, and by the time I'd finished, Guto had finished gathering up the stones on the other side of the field.

Come on, he said, and took hold of the barrow handles as though it was as light as a feather, and rolled it to the rubbish heap near the cowshed, and emptied it. And I was walking alongside and watching everything he did.

Would you like to go for a dip in Swirling Lake?

Dew, yes.

And off we went to Swirling Lake, and stripped naked, and Guto ran about ten yards and dived straight into the middle.

Come on, he said when he surfaced again, wiping water out of his eyes and with his black hair all over his face.

But for a while I stayed sitting by the shallow part with just one foot in the water, shaking like a leaf. Then Guto swam up to me and splashed water over me. Then I dived in, too.

I can't swim, Guto, I said laughing.

Come on, I'll teach you.

And there we were, having fun for ages and ages, with Guto

shouting: Don't be scared, and Come on now, as he tried to teach me how to swim.

I'll teach you properly next time, he said after we'd come out of the water and were sitting in the sun, drying off. And when we were dressed, we went to the house for dinner.

Gel was lying under the table with a big bone, too busy to take notice of anyone.

There was a smell of lobscouse all through the house, and Mam was wearing her apron cos she'd been working with Auntie Ellen, and she was ladling the lobscouse out of a saucepan onto the plates with a cup. When we'd finished eating, there was a big bowlful of bones that had come out of the saucepan, with lots of meat on them. And Auntie Ellen picked up the bowl.

I'll take these out, she said.

Where are you taking them? said Mam.

They're Gel's supper.

Heavens above, don't give give those to the dog, Ellen love. There's too much meat on them. I'll put them in the bag to take home.

And into the bag they went, and poor old Gel had to make do with the bone he had under the table.

After dinner, Guto and me went to pick plums from the tree in the field in front of the house. And within half an hour we had a big basketful, and they were all black, and nice and soft. Guto and me had eaten about a dozen each. We couldn't eat any more cos we'd eaten so much lobscouse.

These are for you and your mam to take home, said Guto. Do you see that field there on the other side of the path? It's packed with bilberry bushes and they're all full of bilberries. We'll go over there picking bilberries next time. We'll go in the hay barn when we've been back to the house, so you can see our hayrick.

And that's where the accident happened.

The Big Field sloped down past the side of the hay barn, and by climbing up the field, we could go in by the top door which was level with the top of the hayrick. But there was a wide gap between the wall and the rick.

Come on, said Guto and jumped straight across the gap onto the top of the hayrick.

Oh, I can't, I said, standing on the edge of the doorway, my nostrils filled with the sweet scent of the hay.

Course you can. Now, jump. I'll catch you.

Alright then, I said, and took a leap. But I didn't reach the top of the rick, or Guto's hand either. And down I went along the side of the rick to the ground floor. And there I was, lying there dazed, and when I opened my eyes I could feel my arm hurting underneath me. And Guto was kneeling by my head.

Are you hurt? his voice said from a long way away.

Lor, I don't know. My arm feels funny.

Try and stand up, then we'll go to the house.

I can't, Guto. This arm's just like a piece of wood.

After looking at my arm and seeing that it was swollen, Guto lifted me up onto his back as though I was a feather and carried me from the hay barn to the house.

He's come a cropper in the hay barn and hurt his arm, Guto told Mam, who'd run out when she saw us passing the window.

You little devil, been up to mischief no doubt, she said when she saw me crying. But she wasn't nasty really cos it was all My little chick this and My little chick that when Guto put me down and I was holding my arm with my right hand. And Mam put me on her knee and started looking at my arm.

Take him to the bedroom, said Auntie Ellen. He'd better go to bed Guto. If he's broken his arm, we'll have to get Doctor Griffiths to set it. You go and get him, Guto.

And Guto shot off like lightning. And Mam helped me get undressed and put me to bed. Dew, it was a fine big bed, too, like the one we had in the bedroom at home. Except that this one was better. I could see the Mountain Path through the window, over the top of the plum tree in the far end of the field in front of the house. And over the fireplace was a big picture of a man's face and he had a black moustache with a black frame round it, with In Loving Memory and a bit of poetry underneath. Mam told me afterwards that it was Uncle Harry, Auntie Ellen's husband, but of course I didn't call him Uncle Harry because he'd died a long time ago.

I went to sleep for the whole afternoon after the doctor came to put my arm in plaster. And I dreamed all sorts of strange things. I'd been for a swim on my own in Swirling Lake and I'd swum like a real expert right across the lake and I was lying flat on my back in the water, looking up at the clouds in the sky. And suddenly, a great big angel flew down from behind a cloud, and he had a black moustache, and landed on the grass at the side of Swirling Lake.

What are you doing in there? he said. You've got no right to bathe in Swirling Lake.

And there I was, swimming across the Lake to the other side and making for the rock where I'd put my clothes but, before I got there, the angel with the black moustache had flown there ahead of me, and taken my clothes. I climbed out of the water and dodged past him and ran away stark naked past the cowshed and up the Big Field to the top door of the barn, and the angel was flying after me. And when I was at the door of the barn, I could feel him breathing down my neck and his moustache tickling my back. And I just took a flying leap and landed smack on my backside on top of the hayrick. And there was the angel standing by the top door, snarling at me from under his black moustache, and I was laughing at him.

Don't you think I can't come after you, he said, and started flapping his wings like a great bird, with my clothes under his arm.

Hey, you can't come over here, I said, pulling faces at him.

Can't I indeed? he said. You watch me.

And he flew over the gap to the top of the rick and fell on top of me. And there we were, rolling in the hay, trying to throw each other like that angel with Jacob that Bob Milk Cart told us about in Sunday School the Sunday before.

And I remember the Bible verse Bob Milk Cart taught us at the time:

And Jacob was left alone; and there wrestled a man with him until the breaking of the day. And when he saw that he prevailed not against him, he touched the hollow of his thigh; and the hollow of Jacob's thigh was out of joint, as he wrestled with him. And he said, I will not let thee go, except thou bless me.

But wow, the angel with the black moustache was much stronger than me, and I couldn't do anything but hold on tight to him, until he grabbed my thigh and made me let go of him. And he threw me to the far side of the hayrick and I fell down into a great bottomless pit, and I kept falling down and down and down without stopping until I opened my eyes and saw Mam standing by the side of the bed with a cup of tea in her hand.

Here you are, chick, she said. You drink this now. Doctor's said you have to stay in bed, so you can stay here with Guto for the week of the holidays. I'm going home now. I'll come and fetch you next week.

I don't want to stay, Mam. I'd rather come home with you. I can walk okay with my arm in a sling.

No, you'd better do what Doctor says. You'll be alright here for a week with Guto. And I'll be back on Wednesday.

I started crying, and I couldn't drink the tea, and I shouted: I want to come with you, Mam.

No, you'd better stop, chick. You stay right where you are, and remember to be a good boy.

And after putting my pillow right and tucking me up and giving me a kiss, Mam turned on her heel and went out through the bedroom door.

Mam, I said, looking for any excuse to bring her back into the bedroom.

What is it, chick? came her voice from the kitchen.

Come here for a little minute.

What's up now?

Who's the man with the black moustache?

That's your Uncle Harry, chick. Auntie Ellen's husband. He's been dead for a very long time.

How can he be my uncle if he's dead?

Now you go to sleep like a good boy, and stop asking silly questions.

133

Then the bedroom door closed.

Mam!

But she didn't answer again. And I lay quietly and listened to them talking in the kitchen, until I heard Mam say: Well, I'm going now. Thanks very much. I'll be back next Wednesday.

I threw the bedclothes off and got up to look through the window. She was just going out of sight past the end of the house in her black frock and her little black hat, dressed as though she'd been to a funeral, except that she had a pink flower on the side of her hat. And the bag was on her arm, full to bursting. Dew, it must be heavy, I said to myself.

She came into sight again as she went down the Hill, walking briskly, and I watched her until she went out of sight again at the bottom of the Hill. I sat at the window for a long time, thinking that I'd be able to see her again coming into sight on the Mountain path, over the top of the plum tree in front of the house. But there was mist on the Mountain and it had started to go dark, and I didn't see her again. And there I was, sitting in the window and looking at the mist and imagining that I could see her walking along the Mountain path, all on her own. Then I went back to bed, miserable, and started crying like a baby with my head in the pillow, completely unable to stop.

When Guto came to bed with me and started talking, I couldn't answer, I just pretended I was asleep so he wouldn't see I was crying. But next morning, when we were having breakfast at the kitchen table, with me with my arm in a sling and eating with one hand, Guto was full of complaints about me.

I didn't get a wink of sleep with him, Mam, he said to Auntie Ellen.

You don't say. What was the matter with him?

Crying in his sleep, he was.

Are you homesick? said Auntie Ellen.

I was sound asleep, I said. I didn't know I was crying.

And shouting, said Guto. And kicking all night. My legs must be black and blue.

You can both go and pick a few bilberries for me today, said

Auntie Ellen, after asking how my arm was. Catrin can make a bilberry tart for tea.

Catrin was eating her breakfast and not speaking to anyone, just staring at my arm in a sling.

Watch his arm, said Aunt Ellen as we were setting off with a little pitcher each to pick bilberries in the field on the other side of the Hill. There was a stile to get over the wall into the field from the Hill, but there was no need to go down the other side, cos the field was level with the top of the wall. Dew, and the place was packed with bilberries when we walked to the far side of the field. It took us hardly any time at all to get a little pitcherful each. And then we sat down in the sun and ate bilberries till our mouths were black. And Guto showed me how to make a necklace out of bilberries and grass stalks.

We'll take it home as a present for Catrin, he said when we'd made a really long one. You can see Snowdon from here, you know. There it is, look, with its head in the clouds.

Lor, I thought Snowdon was a long way away. It's close, isn't it Guto?

Yes, but I bet you can't see the Queen of Snowdon?

Dew, I can't see a queen anywhere. And you can't see one either. You're having me on.

No, honestly. I'm looking at her now. But it's not everybody that can see her.

Is she a real live woman, Guto? I can't see anybody.

No. It's the mountain over there that makes the shape of a woman against the sky, and it's only on clear days like this that she comes into view. She's lying down on the side of the mountain. Now look.

And Guto put one arm around the back of my neck and pointed with his other arm to the mountain next to Snowdon's summit.

Do you see the steep slope over there where the sheep are grazing?

Yes, I see it.

Well, look over that, following my finger, a bit to the left-hand side by the top of the slope. Can you see the shape of a woman's head, lying down?

Yes, I think so.

And then her chest a bit further down.

Yes, I can see it.

And then her belly, all swollen.

Dew, yes.

And then her feet, just showing below her skirt.

Lor, yes. I can see all of her now.

There you are, then. That's the Queen of Snowdon. When you've seen her once, you can always see her after that.

Why do they call her the Queen of Snowdon?

Because she's on top of Snowdon, of course.

Yes, but why do they call her a Queen?

Cos she owns Snowdon, of course. And they say that if she ever gets up and comes down the mountain, it'll be the End of the World.

Lor, can we take these bilberries home now?

Yes, we'll go now. After dinner, you can stay in the house and read while I clean out the cowshed and feed the pig and cut some hay.

Where's that over there, Guto? I said when we stood up, with our backs to Snowdon.

It's Anglesey and Beaumaris and the sea down that way. Hey, Beaumaris is a nice place, boy. It's the finest place in the whole world, Beaumaris.

I can't see any sea, Guto?

No, you can't see the sea from here. You have to go up to the Top of Snowdon to see the sea properly. Or to Beaumaris to be right beside it.

Lor, I've never seen a sea, except in books.

I'll take you on a trip to Beaumaris one day, when you've learned to swim properly. And we'll go for a dip in the sea. And we can sit on the beach and watch the tide come in.

Dew, that was one of the greatest weeks I ever had in my life, going around the Bwlch with Guto, with my arm in a sling. I wasn't the slightest bit homesick after that first night, and Guto didn't complain once that I'd kicked him or been crying in my sleep. And when Mam came to collect me the next Wednesday, I didn't want to go home with her.

Can I stay with Guto for another week, Mam? I said when she'd given me a kiss and asked how my arm was.

No, you'd better come home with me today, she said, so I can fix that old arm for you.

It doesn't hurt at all.

Yes, well you'd better go home with your Mam today, said Auntie Ellen.

And Mam and me were wonderfully happy walking home along the Mountain path that afternoon, with me helping to carry the bag even though I had one arm in a sling.

*   *   *

But it was on the path over the side of the Foel that I saw the sea for the first time ever. It was the year before Canon died, and I was on a trip to Glanaber with the Church Choir. And instead of going all the way on the train, we'd decided to walk over the side of the Foel down to Post Lane and catch the train to Glanaber there. I'd never been on a train before, either.

It was on a Saturday. We all met by the Foel Gate first thing in the morning, and there were more people in the Choir that morning than on any Sunday morning in Church.

Hey, it's a fine day, isn't it? said Huw, who'd arrived before me, with his cheeks all red and smiling from ear to ear. I've brought a bit of bread and butter in my pocket in case we don't get enough to eat.

Me too.

How much money have you got to spend?

Two shillings, and eighteen pence from the Choir.

Dew, we're rich. I've got half a crown in silver threepenny bits. And with the eighteen pence Choir pocket money we're getting in Glanaber, I'll have four shillings. Are you going for a trip on the steamer when we get there?

Yes, if they let us. And I want a donkey ride, as well.

Me too.

And we chatted like that as we went through Foel Gate with the mist rising from the grass and the gorse just as though someone was turning back the bedsheets and there was a green blanket underneath.

When we'd gone halfway up the side of Foel, we were getting tired. Huw had gone ahead with the others, and I was the last in the line, and the others were getting further and further ahead of me. Everyone except Frank Bee Hive and Ceri, Canon's daughter. They were walking together behind the others but ahead of me when the others had gone out of sight over the side of the Foel. I saw Frank put his arm round Ceri's waist, and she pulled his arm away and stopped and started telling him off. Then Frank went ahead on his own, and disappeared from view over the side of the Foel like the others, and Ceri was walking very slowly ahead of me.

Suddenly, she stopped and turned round and saw me coming up. And she walked back to me, with a big smile on her face.

Hello, my boy, she said with a bit of an accent due to being away at school in England. Are you tired?

A bit, I said, puffing like a train and blushing to the roots of my hair.

You hold my hand, she said, and she took hold of my hand with her own. It was soft and lovely and warm. I could walk much faster then and it took us almost no time at all to reach the highest part of the hillside. And it was there that I saw it, the sea for the first time ever, and I stood perfectly still and squeezed Ceri's hand tight.

The view was as though the sky in front of us had suddenly opened like a curtain and revealed the Heavens to us, and the floor of Heaven was like I'd imagined it when I was lying lost on Foel Garnedd looking up into the sky. The floor was the bluest of blues, and the sun was shining on it, and it stretched far far away and then joined the silver wall of Heaven in the far distance. Then, on the left, there was a green carpet of trees in full leaf and the sea was going into it just like the hallway in a great house like the Vicarage. And that one was blue as well, the same colour as the sea. And there was a castle standing on the green carpet and from a distance it looked like a toy one, but it must have been huge when you were standing next to it.

Everything was like I'd imagined it in Church whenever I sang A Better Land in which to Live, and about healthy people without any pain or fear after they crossed the River Jordan. And specially when I was listening to Mam singing as she did the ironing.

> Se-ee beyond the mi-ists of time
>   O-o my s-o-oul behold the view,
>   O-o my s-o-oul behold the view,
>   Whe-e-re the breeze is e-ever tender,
> Whe-ere the sky is e-ever blu-ue,
>   Whe-ere the sky is e-ever blu-ue,
>   Ha-appy pe-eople
>   Ha-appy pe-eople
>   With fa-aces t'ward this pla-ace
>   With fa-aces t'ward this pla-ace.

God lives in that castle, for sure, I said to myself. And Jesus lives there with his Dad now, I bet, fully recovered after being crucified.

I'd let out a gasp when the Heavens opened before me and made me stop and squeeze Ceri's hand. But I didn't know I was crying like a baby until I heard Ceri say: You're tired, aren't you? Let's sit down here for a minute.

No really, I'm happy, I said as I dried my eyes with my coat sleeve, and started laughing. It's just as though we're in Heaven, isn't it?

Ceri put her grey coat down on the dew and sat down, and I sat beside her, and she put her arm round my shoulders, and my head was leaning nicely on her side, and it was soft, just like a pillow, and I could smell her perfume.

Well, I'm in heaven now, anyway, I said to myself.

Do you see that castle down there in the trees? said Ceri.

Lor, yes.

Can I tell you a story about it?

Oh, yes. Is it a true story?

Yes, certainly. How old are you?

I'll be ten in November.

Once upon a time, many years ago, a king lived in that castle and he had one daughter, and she was eighteen years old.

The same age as you, then?

Yes, and one day a wealthy young man came from London to the castle on a white horse, and asked the king for his daughter's hand in marriage. And when she heard her father say Yes you may marry her, she ran upstairs to the highest room in the castle and locked herself in, and her father looked everywhere for her but he couldn't find her. And that night, her sweetheart, a young man with blonde hair and blue eyes, who lived in that great white house over there, on the other side of the river, came very quietly to the castle in the dark and whistled beneath her window. And she made a rope out of the bedclothes and lowered herself down the side of the castle to him. And the pair of them ran away and nobody ever saw them again.

I was just going to sleep listening to Ceri telling the story when she took her arm from around me and made me open my eyes. All the others were down at the bottom, about to disappear into the woods that grew along the side of Post Lane.

We'd better go now, or we'll never catch them up, Ceri said. Can you run?

Course I can.

Down we go then.

And she started down the Foel, running like the wind with her hair billowing out around her head.

And I was flying like a bullet behind her.

13

IT STARTED BADLY, that day after the evening of the South Choir. No wonder it finished worse. It was raining stair rods in the morning and I was sitting in school with wet feet cos my shoes leaked. I couldn't concentrate on what Price the School was trying to say, I just watched the rain hammering against the window as though a lot of evil spirits were crying and wailing, and looked at the great puddles of dirty water in the playground.

Price was giving us Geography, and he'd been drawing a map of Africa on the blackboard and telling us what a hot country it was, full of black people who sometimes ate each other, and the sun beat down on their heads all day, from morning till night. Then he went on to tell us the story of Doctor Livingstone preaching about Jesus to the cannibals and getting lost in the jungle. But my feet were too wet to listen, what with the noise on the window as well. So I put my hand up and asked could I go out to the toilets.

But really I wanted to dry my feet. I had a pair of dry socks in my coat pocket in the cloakroom, and some brown paper to put in my shoes after changing my socks. And after taking off my shoes and changing my socks and putting the brown paper in my shoes and putting them back on again, I found a cigarette end in my waistcoat pocket. I'll go to the toilets for a smoke, I said, even though I'd told Huw the night before that I was never going to smoke ever again.

There I was, creeping along the dry strip under the eaves to the toilets behind the school. Dew, I nearly had a fit when I saw him. There was Will Ellis Porter, lying flat out on the toilet floor, and he had such a great gash in his throat that I thought his mouth was open, and the whole place was swimming in blood. I just took one look at him and ran like the devil to tell Price the School, and I was shaking like a leaf, and he couldn't understand what I was trying to say.

W-W-Will E-E-Ellis P-P-Porter, sir, I said. L-L-Lying ou-ou-outside th-there. H-He's d-dead.

Price shouted for Shorty Williams from Standard Four and they both went out to the toilets. Then we saw Shorty Williams through the window running like lightning across the playing field through the rain without his coat and hat.

Gone to fetch my Dad, said Little Will Policeman.

And Price came in as white as chalk and said we had to go home and there'd be no afternoon school, and no-one was to go near the toilets. Little Will Policeman's Dad had arrived by the time we'd been sent outside, and he was talking quietly by the School door to Price and Shorty, who was soaking wet through.

What did you see? said Huw when we'd crossed the street and were standing in the doorway of the Sixpenny Ha'penny Shop to shelter from the rain and watching to see if we could see them bringing Will Ellis's body out of the toilets.

There he was, lying flat on his back in the toilets, I said, and all the lads were standing around me with their mouths open.

Was he dead? said Johnny Beer Barrel.

Yes. The blood was pouring out of his throat, and his cap had fallen off his head, and his mouth was crooked, and one eye was open as though he was winking at me. And a big knife, like Johnny Edwards Butcher's on the floor beside him, and that was all blood-stained as well.

I was rattling away like a machine gun because talking was the only thing that was stopping me from shaking and I didn't want to let the lads see that I was frightened. And every time I did stop talking, I felt as though I wanted to be sick.

Did he say anything to you? said Davey Corner Shop. He was a daft 'un, young Davey.

Give over, you fool, how could he say anything if he was dead.

He was alright on Saturday, said Johnny Beer Barrel. I saw

him going down the street to the station with a big box on his back.

David Jones', that box, Ann Jones the Shop's brother, going back to America, said Huw.

I saw him last night, said Davey Corner Shop.

Saw who?

Will Ellis Porter, of course. He was on the side of the Braich singing at the top of his voice.

You'll have to go to the quest, Little Will Policeman said to me.

What's a quest?

That's where they say how he died, and decide if he killed himself or if somebody else killed him.

He killed himself, for sure.

How do you know?

It was me that saw him, wasn't it?

Yes, that's why you'll have to go to the quest, so they can question you, so they can decide properly if he killed himself. How do you know someone else didn't take him to the School toilets last night and cut his throat.

Maybe he was drunk, said Davey Corner Shop.

Give over, you fool. How could he get drunk on a Sunday?

And suddenly I thought about Uncle Will, and thought maybe he had killed Will Ellis Porter while he was drunk, and that he'd be hanged. Serve him right as well, I said to myself. Then I told myself Shut up, you fool.

And there we were arguing until it had stopped raining. And all we saw of Will Ellis Porter was Davey Corner Shop's Dad's motor going round the back of the School and being driven away quick as a wink, and Little Will Policeman's Dad sitting in the front with the driver. I couldn't bear the idea of going home on my own.

Are you coming to help me chop sticks in the shed, Huw?

Yes, boy, said Huw. But I've got to be home by dinnertime to see the men from the South Choir before they go away.

Alright then, let's go.

Dew, they're nice men those two South Choir blokes who are

staying with us, said Huw as we went up the Hill. Look what I got off one of them.

And Huw went into his pocket, and brought out a hell of a good pocket knife, not like that one I got from Humphrey Top House ages ago, but a black one with two blades in it, a big blade and a little blade, and both as sharp as razors.

They're not starving, you know, like we thought last night, said Huw. Mam had made a hell of a supper for the two of them but they didn't eat much at all.

Dew, they deserved a proper supper, too, after singing so well.

Telling stories they were, instead of eating. And after supper the two of them sang with us for hours and hours.

Why have they gone on strike?

They want more wages. And they were telling my Dad that they get twice as much as him now, and that they're sure to get the rise, and that the strike will be over in less than a week.

What did your Dad say?

Oh, he was just listening and saying nothing. And they were telling us what a fine place the Rhondda Valley is, where they work, and that they go to Cardiff with their wives, shopping, every Saturday afternoon, just the same as we go down the High Street, and they can go and watch Cardiff City.

Swansea's in the South too, isn't it Huw?

Yes. They were saying that's a fine place as well.

Is it better than Beaumaris?

Yes, and a lot bigger. It's nearly as big as Liverpool.

Never, boy.

That's what they were saying last night, anyway. Dew, people will get a shock when they hear about Will Ellis Porter. What will your Mam say, d'you think?

I don't know, boy.

But by the time we got home, Mam wasn't in the house. She'd left the key under the mat, like she usually did when she went out, so I could get in if I got home before her. And Huw and me went in through the house to the shed in the back.

Look what a good edge there is on this knife, said Huw, sitting on a stool and carving a piece of wood, while I was chopping sticks with the axe. I wonder why Will Ellis Porter killed himself?

He'd gone out of his mind, for sure, I said.

Why do people go out of their minds, d'you think?

They lose control of themselves, you know.

What makes them lose control?

Oh, all kinds of things. Just like you and me get mad sometimes, except they go madder. Look what a mad 'un Moi's Uncle Owen was.

Yes, but he was good to Moi.

But he used to get drunk too. Drunken men are half out of their minds, you know, Huw.

Dew, I'm glad my Dad doesn't get drunk. Do you remember that fight outside The Blue Bell ages ago between Owen Morris Llan and Bob Roberts Ceunant?

I do, boy. Those two were out of their minds with drink as well, you know.

But Will Ellis didn't get drunk.

No he didn't. He used to have fits.

And he didn't know what he was doing when he was having a fit. He must have killed himself while he was in a fit.

He could have done. Do you know who came to our house last night while we were singing with the South Choir?

No?

Uncle Will.

Never, boy.

Yes, and he was drunk. But Mam didn't let him stay with us. She told him to get away from us, just like she did the last time. And she was white and shaking like a leaf when I came home last night. And do you know what I've been thinking, Huw?

No?

You won't tell anybody?

No, I won't, honest.

I've been thinking that Uncle Will killed Will Ellis Porter while he was drunk.

Jesus, I wonder?

He's a wild one, you know, Huw.

He'll get hung if he did.

Serve him right, I'd say.

Where would they hang him, d'you think? In Caernarfon Jail or in Liverpool? There's a big jail in Liverpool.

I don't know what Mam would say.

No, you're imagining things, you know. He had a fit, Will Ellis Porter, I'm sure. Jesus, I'll have to go now or I won't see the South Choir men. I'll see you this afternoon at the end of Lôn Newydd after tea. Bye now.

Bye, Huw.

When I finished chopping sticks, I went out and knocked Next Door to ask if Mam was there.

Is Mam here? I said when Grace Evans came to the door.

No, love, she said. But I saw her going up the Hill this morning. Have you had any dinner?

Yes thanks, Mrs Evans, I said, lying.

I'm sure that old Will Ellis Porter's given you all a fright at School, you poor things. He's an old so-and-so, doing such a thing.

Have you heard, then?

Yes, the coalman's lad told me when he was passing earlier on.

Perhaps Mam's at Top House. I'll go and look there.

Yes, that's where she is, you can be sure.

But Mam wasn't at Top House either. And Lisa Top House said the same as Grace Evans, that she'd seen Mam through the window going up the Hill.

So I went back to the house then and put the saucepan on the fire to heat the lobscouse up. And I put a cloth on the table and plates and bowls and spoons ready for dinner. Maybe Mam's gone to fetch some milk from Tal Cafn so we can have milky potatoes for supper, I told myself. But that'd be strange as well, because I usually bring the milk from Tal Cafn when I've taken the cattle. Or maybe she's gone to Gran's house, and stayed to have dinner with Gran.

Anyway, after waiting for ages, with the lobscouse boiling, I had dinner on my own, and then sat down in the rocking chair to read *The Pilgrim's Progress*. Dew, that was a wonderful book, with great pictures in it. At the time, I'd just started reading it properly, instead of just looking at the pictures, and that afternoon I'd come to the story where Christian goes into the Palace Beautiful, and passes the two lions at the door. But I'd eaten two bowls of lobscouse, and just as Christian passed the two lions, I fell fast asleep in the rocking chair. And instead of seeing the Palace Beautiful, what should I see but Caernarfon Jail.

They'd caught Uncle Will, in my dream, after he'd cut Will Ellis Porter's throat, and he was going to be hanged in Caernarfon that day, and Mam and me had been allowed to go to Caernarfon to watch. Davey Corner Shop's Dad's motor came to fetch us in the morning and when it came up the Hill, Little Will Policeman's Dad was sitting in the front with the driver, and he came with us all the way to Caernarfon, with Mam and me sitting behind. And when we reached Caernarfon, the motor stopped by the door of a big castle.

No, this isn't a castle, said Little Will Policeman's Dad, this is Caernarfon Jail. Come inside.

And in we went along a long narrow passage with no carpet on it, and the men who were in jail were looking at us through railings on each side, just like monkeys in the Lion Show, till we came to the end of the passage and went through another door. And there he was, standing with a rope round his neck, with the hangman standing beside him.

Sit down there, said Little Will Policeman's Dad, and gave us both a chair, and Uncle Will was snarling at us and not saying a word.

Right then, said the hangman's voice. One . . . two . . . three. And the trapdoor opened and Uncle Will disappeared through it with the rope round his neck, without saying a single word.

Serves him right, I said.

But Mam had pulled her hankie out and was crying. He was my brother after all, you know, she said, wiping her eyes.

Then Little Will Policeman's Dad took us for a meal to a big place full of little tables and full of the smell of potatoes and meat. And a nice lady came up to us and asked us what we wanted.

Potatoes and meat, said Mam, and the lady came back smiling all over her face with two big plates full of potatoes and meat. Dew, it was good food too. But Mam was upset and still crying on the way home in the motor, and I was still saying Never mind, Mam. And I was thinking and thinking how I could make her stop crying when I woke up in the rocking chair and *The Pilgrim's Progress* had fallen onto the floor.

The rain was pelting down on the window and it was lightning, and when I looked at the time it was four o'clock, and Mam hadn't come back, and I was shaking like a leaf, frightened to be in the house on my own. But suddenly the rain stopped and within two minutes it was sunshining. I'll go out and see if I can see Huw at the end of Lôn Newydd, I said, and then I'll go to Gran's to see if Mam's there.

Little did I know what Huw had to tell me when I met him at the end of Lôn Newydd.

Jesus boy, Mam got a shock when she heard about Will Ellis Porter, said Huw.

I'm sure she did. My Mam doesn't know yet cos she hasn't come home. I'm going up to Gran's house to fetch her. That's where she is, for sure. Are you coming up Lôn Newydd with me for a walk?

Sure, boy. D'you know those two men from the South Choir who are staying with us? When they came home at dinnertime, they'd had some good news. The Choir had had a telegram saying the strike was over and wanting them to hurry home.

No, boy.

Yes. And Dad had stayed home from the quarry today, and gone out with the two of them and the others to Salem Chapel where they were all meeting to practice. And that's where they were when the telegram came. And do you know what he said when he came back to the house with them?

No, what?

Dew, Mam and me nearly had a fit, boy.

What did he say, then?

He said he was going with them to the South to work in the coal mine.

Never. Did he mean it, as well?

Yes. Mam wasn't happy about it for a long time, and they were arguing all dinnertime. And it was the two South men who persuaded Mam in the end. Dew, they're really nice blokes. Dad'll get twice as much money as he gets in the Quarry, you know. And do you know what else?

No.

By this time, we'd arrived at the Crossroads, and Huw was going down to Stables Bridge, and I was going up Allt Bryn to Gran's. And we'd stopped for a minute by the hedge to talk.

He wants to take me with him, said Huw, looking over the hedge into the field.

You, Huw? I said, and a strange feeling came over me.

Yes, said Huw, still looking into the field.

Will they let you leave school?

Yes, Dad says. Jesus, look, a rabbit.

And there was a rabbit, sitting in the field, staring at us, with its ears stuck up.

Pity I've not got a gun, said Huw.

Will you be able to work in the coal mine, Huw?

Yes, sure thing.

Dew, you'll be talking like Johnny South when you come back.

I'm not coming back.

And there we both were, leaning on the hedge, staring at the rabbit, and I could hear Huw's voice as though he was in a huge tunnel with an echo in it, still saying: I . . . am . . . not . . . coming . . . back. And nobody said a word.

What will your Mam do without the two of you? I said in the end.

Oh, we'll get a house in the South, and she'll move down to us.

When are you going, Huw?

Tomorrow morning, on the eight o'clock train from the station.

Tomorrow?

Yes.

You won't be in School tomorrow, then?

No, boy.

I'll never see you again, then?

I'll write to you when I get there and start working. You'll get the full story, all the details.

Dew, you remember, now.

Course I will. I'd better go now. We've got a lot of packing to do. Bye now, lad, and I will write, honest. And you remember to write to me.

I will, Huw. Goodbye now.

And we shook hands for a long time and kept telling each other to remember to write, then Huw turned back down to Stables Bridge and I set off for Gran's house. But after I'd taken a step or two, I turned round to take another look at Huw before he went out of sight. And he'd turned round too and was running back to me.

Look, he said, when he'd come back to me. You have the knife I got from the South Choir men. There's a great edge on it, you know.

Dew, thanks Huw, I said. Look, you have this knife I've got. It's only a toy, but you'll have lots of fun with it.

I'm sure I will, boy. Well, goodbye then.

Goodbye Huw. Remember to write.

And then we shook hands, and Huw went very slowly down towards Stables Bridge and I stood and watched him till he went out of sight. Then I set off very slowly up Allt Bryn.

It'll be strange in school tomorrow morning without Huw, I said, and started thinking all kinds of things as I went up the Hill. What if he gets killed in the coal mine. I'll never see him again then. But maybe I won't see him again, anyway, after today. And then I remembered that nobody had said who was going to write first, and I was going to run back and ask him, but he was too far away. I won't go to school tomorrow. I'm going to play truant, I said. I couldn't stand being there without Huw being there too. He'll be writing first, of course, because I won't know where to write to. The South's a long way away, too. What will I do now? Huw and Moi have gone, and I'm all on my own. Dew, I was feeling miserable when I got to Gran's.

But things got even worse when I looked through the window and saw Gran sitting in a chair on her own with her glasses on her nose reading the Bible.

Hello Gran, it's me, I said when I'd knocked at the door and gone inside. Has Mam been here?

Eee no, lad. There hasn't been a soul near me all day.

You haven't heard about Will Ellis Porter then?

Heard what?

Killed himself.

Heavens above, no. Where?

Behind the School. It was me that found him, lying on the floor with his throat cut this morning. And Price the School sent us all home. But when I got home, Mam wasn't there.

She's not come home since morning? said Gran, closing the Bible and standing up, and looking at me in a strange way.

No. And she wasn't in Grace Evans' or in Lisa Top House's, and they'd both seen her going up the Hill this morning. But she's sure to have come home by now.

I'd better come up with you, said Gran, and she went to get her hat and cape. You wait, I won't be two minutes.

And off we went, Gran and me, back home. Dew, it was lucky that Gran came with me too cos I don't know what I would have done if I'd walked into the house and seen her like that. It was lucky that Gran went in first, too, cos I would have got an even bigger shock than when I saw Will Ellis Porter lying in the toilets with his throat cut. Cos there was Mam sitting in the chair with no hat on and her hair all over the place, and still wearing her coat and she was soaking wet.

What is it, Mam? Where've you been? I said and ran to her to give her a kiss. But she took no notice of me, she just looked through me with her steel pin eyes, like she did that other night, and she was mumbling and really going on at someone she thought was standing behind her.

You go next door and ask Grace Evans to come here straight away. Your Mam's not well, said Gran, taking her hat and cape off. I shot out like lighting. They'd just finished their Quarry supper Next Door.

You wait here, lad, said Grace Evans when I told her. Make him a cup of tea, Ellis. And there's some bread and butter for you on the plate. I'll be back soon.

He was a quiet bloke, Ellis Evans, with his nose in his paper all the time. And after pouring a cup of tea for me, he sat down and went back to his paper. And I was gobbling up the bread and butter.

She looked awful, I said.

Who looked awful? he said.

Mam.

It's a weakness that's come on her, you know. She hasn't been well for a long time, so our Grace says.

Have you heard about Will Ellis Porter?

Gawd, yes. I wasn't at all surprised when our Grace told me. He always was a strange one, Will Ellis. And those old fits of his had been getting worse. How old was he, d'you know? He must have been around the fifty mark. I'll get the full story in the paper next week.

I'd better go now to see if they need the doctor fetching, or something.

No, lad. You stay here till Grace comes back. She'll say what's to be done. Have another piece of bread and butter.

By this time, it was seven o'clock and still belting down with rain, and it'd gone dark early because of the storm. Dew, I thought they were lucky Next Door. A great blazing fire and the kettle singing quietly on the hob and the cat sitting by the fender in front of the fire purring away, and Ellis Evans sitting in the armchair in his stocking feet reading his paper, and a nice smell of tobacco smoke coming from his pipe.

Dew, Mrs Evans is a long time, I said. Maybe I'd better go home now.

No, it's best for you to stay here like she said. She won't be much longer.

Alright then, I said. But every minute seemed like an hour as I sat at the table trying to make every piece of bread and butter last as long as possible and listening to the clock pendulum going to and fro tick . . . tock . . . tick . . . tock as though nothing had happened all day.

You go home now, lad, said Grace Evans when she eventually came back. Your Mam's in bed now and she wants to see you. And afterwards you can go down and fetch Doctor Pritchard, but you're to say to Doctor Pritchard that your Mam's really ill and that her and Gran are asking him to come. Do you understand, now?

Yes, Mrs Evans.

And I was out through the door as quick as a wink. And there was Mam lying in bed as white as chalk and looking at me in a strange sort of way, but not saying anything. And Gran was with her in the room.

Did Grace Evans tell you what to say? said Gran.

Yes. I'll go now.

And out I went through the rain to fetch the doctor, with my feet soaking wet cos my shoes leaked and the water had gone through the brown paper.

I had to wait a long time to see Doctor Pritchard cos there were a lot a sick people there before me waiting to see him. And by the time I'd seen him and walked home again, it was nine o'clock. And Gran was in the kitchen washing dishes.

Doctor Pritchard says he'll be here between ten and eleven, I said.

Alright, said Gran. Your Mam's asleep now. You'd better go to bed now or you won't be able to get up in the morning. I'm going to stay here tonight. Here, take this before you go upstairs.

And she put some powder in a glass and poured hot water from the kettle onto it, and stirred it with a spoon.

You drink that straight back now, she said.

Eeeerch, what was it? I said when I'd swallowed it. Assifetta?

No. Medicine in case you get a cold. Hurry up to bed now.

And upstairs I went, and I was in bed the second I'd dried my feet. And I just had enough time to look through the roof window and see that the moon had drowned in the clouds before I fell into a deep, deep sleep.

14

THE FIRST THING I saw when I woke up and opened my eyes next morning was a spider on the skylight trying to get out through the window, but it was closed. There he was walking along the glass upside down, walking for a while and falling, and going back and walking and falling again. But he never fell onto the floor cos there was a thread just like elastic holding him whenever he fell, and that's how he could get back on the window each time.

It had only just gone six, and I was about to go and fetch the cattle from Tal Cafn. And suddenly, while I was lying there watching the spider, I remembered about Huw. In less than two hours, Huw would have set off for the South and maybe I'd never see him again. And I wouldn't be able to go to the station to see him after fetching the cattle cos Mam was ill.

Dew, yes, Mam as well. I'd forgotten about her. I'd slept so soundly after that powder Gran had given me that I'd forgotten everything, and I hadn't dreamt about anything all night. But Jesus, I'd dreamed enough in the afternoon to last me a lifetime. Sometimes, you dream backwards like I did about that angel with the black moustache, after seeing Uncle Harry's picture when I was lying in Guto's bed. And sometimes you dream forwards, like when I dreamt about us going in the motor to Caernarfon Jail to see Uncle Will get hanged, with Little Will Policeman's Dad sitting in the front with the driver. But little did I think that the dream would come true so soon.

Our house was as quiet as the grave when I got out of bed and got dressed to go and fetch the cattle. But when I'd gone downstairs and opened the door to go out, I heard the sound of a cat miaowing. Grace Evans Next Door's cat must have been left out all night, I said. But I went back and listened outside Mam's bedroom door, where her and Gran were sleeping, and that's where the sound was coming from. Grace Evans' cat wasn't there at all, I said. It's Mam crying in her sleep. And I went out and closed the door very quietly after me.

It was drizzling and it looked like the rain had set in for the day. It was as black as night at the top of Nant Ycha and the the clouds were just like steam coming out of a washing tub full of boiling water. But it was daylight by the top of the Foel with the mist rising from the ground and climbing slowly up the side of the Mountain as though it was tired. I must take my shoes to Cwt Crydd to be mended today, I said, but I was enjoying the feel of the drizzle washing my face cos I hadn't had a wash before I came out. After crossing the Gorlan Potato Field, I climbed up on top of the Corn Field wall to see if there were any mushrooms there. And there they were, like white spots all over the place, as though the Tan Fron chickens had been busy laying eggs all night. Dew, I'll have a capful of those on the way home, I said as I got down from the wall. And I did get a capful, too.

Gran was up by the time I got back to the house, and the kettle was on the fire.

Look what a good capful of mushrooms I've got, Gran, I said. How's Mam this morning?

She's asleep. Don't you go into the bedroom disturbing her, said Gran. You get those mushrooms ready for frying, then you can have your breakfast.

Did Doctor Pritchard come last night? I said from the back kitchen as I cleaned the mushrooms.

Yes.

What did he say?

I'll tell you in a minute. Wait till I've made breakfast.

I don't want to go to School today, Gran. I'd rather stay at home to help.

Aye, you'd better not go to School today. There's a lot to be done.

Gran didn't say anything for ages when we sat at the table to have breakfast. She was forever up and down doing something, slicing bread or filling the teapot or poking the fire. It was as though she couldn't stay still for a minute, and she didn't speak a word.

Dew, these mushrooms are good, I said in the end. Is Mam very ill?

Yes. She's quite poorly.

When does Doctor Pritchard say she can get up?

There was silence then for a while. Then Gran got up from the table once again and turned to the fire and put the kettle on it. Then she turned to me and said: Look, your Mam'll be waking up in a minute, and there'll be a lot do do. Doctor Pritchard says she has to be taken to hospital, and you'll need to go with her.

How are they taking her to hospital with her ill in bed? Is there an ambulance coming to fetch her?

No. It's the Corner Shop Motor that's coming.

The Corner Shop Motor?

Yes, lad. Look, you've to go Next Door now. Ellis Evans has stayed home from the Quarry today and he and Grace Evans will tell you what wants doing. You go now, lad, and I'll go into the bedroom and see if your Mam's woken up. You go off Next Door now.

Even though Gran was speaking more kindly to me than she usually did, there was something in her voice that made me keep my mouth shut and do what she said without asking any more questions. And there was no need to ask anything else once I went Next Door. I found out more than I wanted to know there.

Come in love, said Grace Evans when I knocked on the door, and she was talking much kinder than usual, just like Gran.

Come up to the fire, said Ellis Evans, in his stocking feet and about to light his pipe after breakfast. Have you had your breakfast?

Yes thanks, I said. A big plateful of fried mushrooms from the Gorlan Corn Field.

How's your Mam this morning?

She was asleep when I came out. Gran says she's really poorly and they want to take her to hospital. But they want to take her in the Corner Shop Motor, but I want to know why she can't go in an ambulance with her being so ill.

Well yes, lad. That's what we want to talk to you about, said Grace Evans, pulling her chair from the table to the fire. You want to go with her, don't you?

That's what Gran was saying. But why are they taking her in the Corner Shop Motor with her being so ill?

She isn't ill in the way you mean, love, said Grace Evans.

She's in a weakness, you know, said Ellis Evans, blowing tobacco smoke up the chimney and thumbing his pipe.

They'll be very kind to her.

They'll look after her properly.

She's sure to be better in no time.

She won't be there long, you know.

And they went on like this for ages, one after the other, until my head was spinning. And I didn't understand what they were talking about until I asked: They'll be taking her to Bangor, then?

No, you see, they both said together, and Ellis Evans coughed and cleared his throat after blowing some more smoke up the chimney. Then he put his hand on Grace Evans' knee and turned to me.

Do you know where your Mam was yesterday? he said.

No.

Well, from all accounts, she'd gone up the Hill in the morning and had been wandering on the side of the Foel all day.

Good God, and it was pouring down.

Yes. Robin Gorlan saw her passing Tan Fron about twelve o'clock, and Owen Gorlan had seen a woman on Pen y Foel at about three in the afternoon. She was too far away for him to recognise her properly but he swears it was your Mam.

Good God, I said again, and started shaking like a leaf.

Will you have a cup of tea? said Grace Evans. There's a nice cuppa left in the teapot, here.

No, no thanks. What happened then?

Well, nobody knows for certain, said Ellis Evans, tapping his pipe on the chimney corner. But the next time anyone saw her, she was walking down Allt Bryn past the Lockup.

What time was it by then?

About five, probably. And do you know what she did then?

No.

Threw a stone through the Lockup window.

Who? Mam?

Yes.

No.

Yes, honestly.

No, you're just joking.

It's as true as I'm sitting in this chair.

And although I was shaking like a leaf, I started to roar with laughter, with the pair of them staring at me.

Dew, I just can't stop laughing, I said. Mam, of all people, throwing a stone through the Lockup window.

Well, that's what happened, said Ellis Evans. And our Grace saw her coming up the Hill about half past five, and she looked so bad that Grace went to see what she could do. But your Mam was telling somebody off something terrible, you know, and talking about your Uncle Will, wasn't she Grace?

Yes, said Grace Evans. And when I went to ask if there was anything I could do for her, she went into the house and slammed the door in my face.

She's been talking funny for days, you know, said Ellis Evans. She has, hasn't she?

What she was saying coming up the Hill, said Grace Evans, was that your Uncle Will had been hanged in the Lockup.

Dew, my dream's coming true.

What dream, lad?

Oh, nothing.

And suddenly I understood everything.

They want to take her away, don't they? I said, looking into the fire. And though nobody spoke the words, they were racing through my head like the little Quarry train. Denbigh. The Asylum. They're taking Mam to the Asylum, the Asylum, the Asylum. Emyr, Little Owen the Coal's Brother. In his coffin with his mouth open. Beaten and battered. Emyr thirsty. They'll be very kind to her. She's in a weakness. Uncle Will being hanged. Throat pouring with blood. The Asylum. The Asylum. The Asylum.

Drink this while it's hot now, lad.

No thanks, Mrs Evans. I can't swallow. I'd better go now, to see if she's up.

By this time, Ellis Evans was busy putting his boots on. And when he'd finished, he got up and came over to me and put his hand on my shoulder, and called me old chap for the first time ever.

You listen to me, old chap, he said. This is a pretty trying time for all of us, but we've got to accept whatever God sends us, you know. And we've got to make the best of things as they are.

Don't frighten the lad, Ellis, said Grace Evans. His Mam's just a bit fragile at the moment. She'll be back home good as new in about a fortnight, for sure, as long as everyone does right by her.

You let me speak, Grace, said Ellis Evans really sharply, then he turned back to me. We'll do everything we can to help, but we're depending on you now, see.

I'll do everything that needs doing.

That's it. The Corner Shop Motor will be at the bottom of the Hill at half past nine, and you'll have to take your Mam down the Hill to it. Maybe she won't be all that keen to go, but you'll have to persuade her.

I know what to do.

That's it, lad. You go now. It's quarter past nine.

Alright then.

And tell your Gran to come here when you've gone.

I will, Mrs Evans, I said, and out I went.

Hello, Mam, are you better? I said in a high voice as I went into the house. And there she was, sitting in the rocking chair, dressed, and Gran was brushing the chimney corner and taking the kettle off the fire. But Mam didn't say anything, she just looked at me as though I'd been stealing apples.

Dew, Gran made me a good breakfast, I said then, as though nothing was wrong. A big plateful of mushrooms.

159

Where've you been? she said, looking at me with her steel pin eyes.

Just to fetch the cattle and then to Next Door to see if Grace Evans wanted anything. Huw and his dad have gone away to the South on the eight o'clock train, and I'm not going to school today. You and me are going for a ride in the Corner Shop Motor because we're on holiday. You'd better put your best hat on, Mam.

Yes, you'd better wear that black hat, said Gran.

And she got up without saying a word and went to the bedroom to get her hat.

Gran ran to the window and looked outside.

They're there, she said to me, quietly.

I'm ready now, said Mam, coming out of the bedroom with her best hat on.

We'll go then, I said, when I'd put my topcoat on and got my cap from the back kitchen.

Grace Evans wants you to call Next Door for a minute, I said to Gran as we were going out and she was standing in the doorway watching us go down the Hill.

It was still drizzling, and I was holding Mam's arm in case she slipped and thinking about the first time we ever walked down the Hill together, long ago. It was her that was holding my arm then. It was a freezing cold day in the middle of winter and everywhere was frozen solid and I was going back to School after being ill with a cold. And the Hill was shining like glass and we were walking by the side of the wall in case we fell over. Mam was holding onto the wall and I was holding onto her arm. And we'd both put a pair of socks over our shoes, so we wouldn't slip. But I fell over twice, and Mam lifted me up each time I fell.

Good God, my dream's coming true again, I said to myself and squeezed Mam's arm even tighter when we got to the bottom of the Hill and saw the Corner Shop Motor.

Who was sitting in the passenger seat in his ordinary clothes but Little Will Policeman's Dad and Little Davey Corner Shop's Dad was standing by the car, holding the door open for us and smiling from ear to ear.

Here we are at last, he said. I hope you're not wet. Fairly middling weather we're having, isn't it?

And into the car we went, and Davey Corner Shop's Dad shut the door behind us and went back to the front end, to the driver's seat next to Little Will Policeman's Dad. And who was sitting in the back with us in the far corner but a lady I'd never seen before. I'm coming with you as well, she said, and smiled at us nicely.

And Mam started roaring with laughter. What are you doing with us, you old devil? she said to Little Will Policeman's Dad. It was you who hanged my Brother Will, wasn't it?

He didn't say anything. He just turned his head towards us and half smiled. Then everyone was quiet for a long time, and the car was going like the wind. And the only talking there was, was Mam talking to herself or to someone she thought was behind her, and laughing and arguing in turn.

Dew, those people from the South are good singers, Mam, I said in the end. You didn't hear the South Choir singing on the side of the Headland on Sunday night, did you? Dew, it was just like the Revival there, with all the people singing with the choir and not being able to stop, they'd got themselves worked up to such a pitch. Dew, you should have heard them singing The Man who was Crucified Long Ago.

Then Mam started singing while I was still talking to her, so I started singing along with her, with the motor still going like a bat out of hell.

Dew, Mam had got carried away too, and I was singing bass with her cos my voice had broken. And the two in the front were still talking to each other and taking no notice of us at all. And there we were, Mam and me singing at the tops of our voices:

> The Man who was crucified long ago
>   For a sinful man like me
> who drained the cup completely
>   Himself on Calvary

By this time, the two in the front had stopped talking and the next thing I heard was the pair of them singing with us, with

161

Little Will Policeman's Dad singing tenor. And then the five of us, the nice lady as well, were singing:

> The source of Everlasting Love
>> That peaceful home all minds do crave
> Takes me to that covenant
>> Ne'r broke by death nor broke by grave

And Little Will Policeman's Dad struck it up then and everyone was getting more and more emotional until I almost forgot where we were going. But everyone went quiet after that, and the sound of the engine was making me feel sleepy. And I had a bit of a doze as we went along the road, listening to Mam talking to herself and then telling someone off and then talking to herself . . .

At last we came to a big gate by the side of the road and the Corner Shop Motor turned through it and went along a wide gravel drive to the door of a huge building about four times as big as Salem Chapel, with stone steps on each side going up to the door.

The Asylum, I said to myself.

Davey Corner Shop's Dad came to open the motor car door for us, and Little Will Policeman's Dad stayed exactly where he was, not moving from his seat. Mam was shaking like a leaf as she got out of the car, but she didn't say anything, and the nice lady was very gentle with her.

You come with me now, she said, taking her by the arm. We'll go and see the doctor and everything will be alright.

And I walked behind them like a pet lamb.

There was a man in a white coat waiting for us at the door when we'd gone up the stone stairs, and he was nice too and he was smiling a big, friendly smile as he welcomed us.

Come through here and sit down while I go and fetch the nurse, he said, and he took the nice lady and Mam and me to a place like a parlour, with lots of chairs in a single row against the wall, and a table in the middle with a flower pot on it, full of flowers; and a big window that nobody could see through on the left-hand side, and a big cupboard on the right-hand side with two doors in it. And the three of us sat down on the chairs to wait.

And we waited there for a long time, and the only thing that happened was that Mam told the nice lady that she wanted to go to the toilet. You come with me, she said kindly, I'll show you where it is. And out they went and left me sitting on my own.

Then this little fat man came in and went to the cupboard without taking any notice of me. And when he tried the door, it was locked, and he started to look in his pocket for the key. He tried his trouser pocket first but it wasn't there; then his waistcoat pocket then his coat pocket and then his inside pocket. But the key mustn't have been there cos he went out again without opening the cupboard door.

Dew, he looked just like Uncle Will, I said to myself. But I was imagining things, of course.

When Mam and the nice lady came back and sat down, a pretty little girl in a nurse's uniform, about the same age as me, came in and gave us a big smile. Dew, she was a pretty little thing too, with blonde hair and blue eyes and rosy cheeks, and when she smiled at us her teeth were shining white. And she had a lot of keys hanging on a piece of string in her hand. She was exactly like Little Jini Pen Cae.

Will you come with me, please? she said to Mam and the nice lady, taking no notice of me. And they went with her and I stayed where I was.

I was feeling really downhearted by this time. I never thought the Asylum would be a place like this, I said to myself. I was expecting to see lots of crazy people. And then suddenly I heard a scream from behind the window and then someone started laughing. I stood up and went to the window and started thinking about poor old Emyr. But I couldn't see through the window. It's just someone messing about, I said, and went back to my chair and sat down.

After a bit, who came in again but the little fat man, and he went straight to the cupboard the same as before, without looking at me. He started looking in his pockets for the key again, only this time time he found it in his waistcoat pocket. And when he'd opened the cupboard, he started taking all sorts of rubbish out of it and putting it all in a pile on the floor. It was as though he was looking for something but he couldn't find it. And when he'd taken everything out of the cupboard, he put it all back really neatly and locked the door again. Then he put the key in his pocket and started to walk out of the room. But when he got to the door, he stopped and turned round to look at me. Then he walked back to me slowly and looked at me very strangely.

Do you know who I am? he said.

No, I don't, I said.

Jesus Christ's brother-in-law, he said.

Dew, I got a shock. I didn't know what to do, run out through the door or laugh in his face.

Oh really? I said in the end.

But he didn't say anything else, he just turned on his heel and headed for the door again. And when he reached the door he turned round with a perfectly straight face and said: In my Father's house there are many mansions.

And out he went.

And I just burst out laughing.

But my mouth snapped shut like a mousetrap when another man came into the room and went to the cupboard. This one was tall and thin and his eyes looked like they were sinking back into his head. He just looked at the cupboard, then turned and came over to me.

Did you see that man who just came in? he said.

Yes, I said.

He's not a full shilling, you know.

Isn't he?

No, he's not even a threepenny bit, really.

And then he went out, too. I got up and went back to the window and looked all over to see if I could find a hole in the white paint, so I could see through. But there wasn't one and I couldn't see anything. So I went back and sat down again and waited. And I was still chuckling about the two funny men, the short fat one and the tall thin one.

At last, the nice lady came back in, on her own, carrying something in her hand.

Here you are, she said. You'll have to take this home with you.
And she put a little parcel, tied with string, in my hand.
What is it? I said.
Your Mam's clothes. And these, too. You'll have to take these, too.
And she put two rings in my other hand. One was Mam's wedding ring, which had worn very thin, and the other ring was the one she always wore with the wedding ring.
I couldn't speak. I just looked at the little parcel in my right hand and the two rings in my left. And I tried to think how they'd got all Mam's clothes into such a small parcel.
And then I started crying. Not crying like I used to years ago whenever I fell down and hurt myself; and not crying like I used to at some funerals either; and not crying like when Mam went home and left me in Guto's bed at Bwlch Farm ages ago.
But crying just like being sick.
Crying without caring who was looking at me.
Crying as though it was the end of the world.
Crying and screaming the place down, not caring who was listening.
And glad to be crying, the same way some people are glad when they're singing, and others are glad when they're laughing.
Dew, I'd never cried like that before, and I've never cried like that since, either. I'd love to be able to cry like that again, just once more.
And I was still screaming and crying as I went out through the door and down the stone steps and along the gravel drive and through the gate onto the road, until I sat down by the side of the road by the gate. Then I stopped crying and started groaning, just like a cow groans when she's having a calf, then I started screaming and crying again.
And there I was, crying and groaning, and groaning and crying when the Corner Shop Motor came along to where I was sitting, and Little Will Policeman's Dad got out and put me in the back with the nice lady. And when I'd laid there groaning for a while, with the motor flying like the wind, the sound of the engine sent me sound asleep. And I slept all the way home.

15

DEW, I WISH I could have her company now, her holding my hand and me with my arm round her, and both of us walking together up to Black Lake. If it was six o'clock at night instead of six in the morning, I'd think it was the same evening, too. Except that I won't be running into Little Jini Pen Cae, like I did that evening.

It was only a year since they'd taken Mam away, and the Summer holidays had started and I'd left school, and Gran wanted me to go and work in the Quarry and I didn't want to go.

It's time you were earning your keep now, you know, Gran said to me as she cut the bread for tea that evening. Ellis Evans says you can go with him tomorrow and start.

I don't want to go to the Quarry, Gran. I'd rather be a servant boy on a farm like Robin. I can get a job at Tal Cafn if I go and ask. And if I can't, I want to be a sailor like Humphrey Top House.

Oh, be quiet, you little devil. You and your sailors. You'll do what I tell you, and go to the Quarry with Ellis Evans tomorrow morning, or I'll know the reason why not.

We'll see about that, I said, and I put my cap on and went out and slammed the door behind me.

I was out with Robin Gorlan every night after Huw went to the South with his Dad. I'd never got a letter from Huw like he promised, and all we knew about him was that his Mam had moved out of Stables Bridge Terrace and gone to live with them in the South.

But Robin wasn't home that afternoon and nobody knew where he'd gone. So I went up Post Lane for a walk. I'll go up to Black Lake, I said. Maybe Robin's gone there fishing.

But instead of Robin, who did I see coming towards me there but Little Jini Pen Cae. I got a shock when I recognised her, cos the last thing I'd heard about her was that they'd taken her away after she'd been with Emyr, Little Owen the Coal's Brother, in Braich Woods. But there she was, as large as life, in a blue frock and holding a little blue hat with white ribbons on it, and her blonde hair was shining in the sun. She was exactly like that girl I saw when we took Mam away, and her teeth were white, gleaming white, when she laughed.

Hello, how are you? I haven't seen you for ages, she said, and her blue eyes were laughing at me. Have you left school?

Yes, I've just left. Well, fancy meeting you here.

I'm at Black Lake Farm. Hey, it's a lovely night, isn't it?

Oh yes. Where are you going?

For a walk, into the Village. Where are you going?

For a walk, to Black Lake. Well, I was.

And we both went to the side of the road and leaned on the gate to look at the sheep grazing in the field. There was another field beyond that one, and another after that. And the last one was full of rushes going down to the River as it flowed very slowly through the flatland and twisted like a snake till it disappeared in the middle of Braich Woods in the distance. And there was the mountain, just like it is now, reaching up into the sky.

This field belongs to Black Lake Farm, doesn't it? I said.

Yes, and the other two that go down to the River, as well. All these fields all around us belong to Black Lake Farm, and all those all the way to Black Lake.

Dew, they must be very rich, the people at Black Lake Farm.

They are. And they're nice people, too. Would you like to come for a walk to the Riverbank over the fields?

Dew, yes.

Help me over this gate, then. If you hold this hat, I can climb over on my own.

Alright, then.

While I was standing with her hat in my hand and making

sure she didn't fall, she lifted one leg over the gate and I could see all her underskirt, and half her bare thigh. And she was so wonderful, sitting there on top of the gate, looking down at me and laughing at me with her blue eyes and white teeth, and her hair shining in the sun.

I'll take the hat now, so you can get up, she said, taking her hat and jumping down into the field. And I jumped after her.

It's lovely over there, down by the River, she said. I go there all the time when I take Toss for a walk.

Who's Toss?

The dog from Black Lake Farm, of course.

Is that Black Lake Farm over there then, where Black Lake goes out of sight?

Yes, didn't you know?

I wasn't quite sure. But I went there once, ages ago. I'd got lost picking bilberries and went to ask for a glass of water. And I got a glass of milk and a big slice of bread and butter from the lady. Dew, yes, they must be nice people. How old's Toss?

Oh, he's just a puppy. He's only six months old.

It wasn't him I saw that time, then. That Toss was fourteen.

Oh yes, he died, that one.

The rushes had grown high in the field closest to the River and we had to watch where we were going in case we lost the sheep track. But Jini knew her way okay, and I kept close behind her. She was bending forward a little as she went through the rushes and her hair had parted into two long plaits and they were falling one each side over her shoulders and her breasts. And she hadn't closed two buttons on the back of her frock near her neck and a bit of her back was bare. And the frills on her petticoat were showing under her blue frock as she bent forward, and her legs looked more shapely from behind than they had when I was looking at her when I'd met her on Post Lane. And her wonderful smell mixed with the lovely smell of the grass and the rushes was making it hard for me to breathe. And when I thought she was going to trip, I put both arms out and grabbed her.

Watch you don't fall, I said.

Ah, don't tickle me, she said, and the sound of her laughter filled the air. And she started running towards the Riverbank, and the two white ribbons on her hat were flying in the air. And I ran after her.

When we reached the clearing by the Riverbank, she threw herself onto the ground and turned over, flat on her back, with both her arms out, and her little blue hat in her right hand, and her legs wide apart too and her skirt up to her knees and her petticoat showing.

Dew, it's hot, she said, and blew a strand of blonde hair away from her face. Come and lie down.

And I lay down on my back beside her.

The sky was blue like it was when I was lying on my back in the bilberry bushes on top of Foel Garnedd ages ago. But I didn't think about Heaven's floor this time. I saw the sky full of blue eyes laughing at me, and every one of them was Little Jini Pen Cae's. And it wasn't as quiet as it had been on the top of Foel Garnedd either, the River was making a lovely sound like lots of people talking to each other all around us and saying the same thing over and over again. And I remembered the huge pendulum on Next Door's clock going tick . . . tock . . . tick . . . tock as though nothing had happened that day. And I could hear Jini breathing by my side, out of breath after running.

Can you swim? she said, eventually.

Course I can. I could swim when I was ten. My cousin Guto taught me to swim in Swirling Lake at Bwlch Farm ages ago. Dew, he was a strong lad, Guto.

You're a strong lad too, aren't you?

Yes, fairly strong. Can you swim?

I can a bit. Enough to cross the River.

And Jini sat up with a straw between her teeth. Do you see Pen Rallt Wen over there, on the other side of the River?

Yes, I said, still lying down and staring up into the sky. And all I could see was thousands of blue eyes laughing at me.

Do you fancy a race with me across the river and up to Pen Rallt Wen?

How will we get across the River?

Dive in, of course, and swim.

169

And get soaked to the skin?

We'll take our clothes off, of course. Nobody'll see us from Post Lane. The rushes will hide us.

And run up Rallt Wen stark naked?

Yes, of course, she said, and leaned down to me and put her two soft hands on my face. Yes, of course, she said very slowly. Yes, of course, stark . . . naked.

And I took hold of her and turned her onto her back and started kissing her like someone who'd gone mad. And she put her arms around me and squeezed me tight. And after we'd been like that for a long time, she let go of me and started pushing me off her. But her rosy cheeks were as red as fire.

Dew, I would have been out of breath before I got halfway to the top of Rallt Wen, she said, and we lay there with our heads close together. When did you leave School?

Yesterday, when School broke up. They want me to go to work in the Quarry and I want to be a farm boy or else go to sea.

Why don't you be a farm boy at Black Lake Farm? They want a farm boy there.

Dew, yes. Do they really?

Yes, really.

We could be together every night then.

That's right.

And come here all the time.

That's right.

And race across the River.

That's right.

After taking our clothes off.

Yes.

Stark naked.

Yes.

You undressing me and me undressing you.

Yes.

Like this.

And like this.

And like this.

She was the only girl I ever had.

But they were lying when they said that I'd thrown Little Jini Pen Cae into the River when they found her clothes on the Riverbank. The last thing I remember is seeing her sleeping quietly and I started thinking about Price the School taking her through that door in School and Em, Little Owen the Coal's Brother taking her to Braich Woods. And I was looking at her and thinking she was such a pretty little thing, and she had such a soft little throat, as white as linen, and her cheeks were red and as hot as fire. And putting my hands round her throat and kissing her as she slept, and starting to squeeze her.

It was terribly late when I got home that night, and Gran had gone to bed. But I'd decided what to do. I'd decided that I was never going to go to that damned old Quarry with Ellis Evans Next Door. I was going to run away to sea like Humphrey Top House did when he was a boy and like Arthur Tan Bryn when he ran away to join the army when the War was on. If Huw could go to the South and get work in a coal mine, I could go to Liverpool and get work on a ship. The only thing was, I only had a shilling in my pocket, but Liverpool wasn't as far as the South and if I started walking along Post Lane past Glanaber I'd be sure to get a lift from someone.

I went into the back kitchen to fetch the bread from the breadbin and I cut lots of slices and wrapped them in paper and put them in my overcoat pocket, and put my cap back on. But before putting the light out and going out, I took the candle to the mantelpiece to have one more look at the picture. It was a picture of Mam and Gran that had been taken on the day of Auntie Ellen's funeral. And the two of them were standing there dressed in black, with Mam looking young beside Gran, wearing that little black hat with the flat brim, like Hughes the Parson's hat. And even though they were both smiling at the photographer, it was easy enough to see that their eyes were still full of tears from the funeral.

And poor Gran, looking so old. She'd been very good to me since they took Mam away, even though we were always rowing. She'd be sure to worry in the morning, seeing my bed not slept in and not knowing where I was. I'd better leave her a little note, I said. And I found a piece of paper and wrote:

Don't worry about me, Gran. I've gone away to work, just like Huw. I'll come back one day with a lot of money and buy you loads of posh clothes.

Then I put the note on the table with the bread knife on top of it in case the wind blew it onto the floor. And went to the mantelpiece once more before snuffing the candle.

Oh, I'll take this with me, I said, and shoved the picture into my inside pocket.

I could make out the Lockup Clock in the light of the street lamp as I went down the Street. It was half past two. But everywhere else was as dark as could be. But I could have walked as far as the Sheep Field with my eyes shut, cos I knew every single paving stone on both sides of the Street, and every lamp post and every telegraph pole, and every grid. And I knew where the pavement stopped and where it started again, and where Post Lane started without any pavement at the start of Lôn Newydd.

I wasn't a bit scared either as I got to the Sheep Field, like I used to be years before with Huw and Moi, or on my own, whistling like a fool as I went by in case I saw a ghost or a bogeyman. And it was nice to be able to leave the Village in the dark, without seeing the shops or the School or the Church or any houses or anything. Because if I'd left in daylight, they'd have made me feel too homesick and maybe I would have broken my heart before I even got to the Sheep Field and turned round and gone to work in the Quarry with Ellis Evans.

I was okay once I'd passed the Sheep Field, cos it wasn't so dark then, and I was walking so quickly that I'd reached Glanaber before I realised where I was. And I was thinking how fine it would be to go on a ship and see the sea, and remembering how I saw it for the first time from the top of the Foel, sitting with Ceri. And I wouldn't have been caught either if that man who gave me a lift outside Glanaber hadn't asked where I was from and then stopped his lorry near Liverpool to speak to a policeman.

* * *

Streuth, Black Lake at last. Someone must have pulled this wall down, cos I used to have to climb on top of it to see Black Lake, and now it only comes up to my knees. And I can see over it kneeling down like this. Ooh, my feet hurt. I'll take these old shoes off for a minute or two.

Jees, the old Lake looks good too. It's strange that they call it Black Lake cos I can see the sky in it. Blue Lake would be a better name for it, cos it looks as though it's full of blue eyes. Blue eyes laughing at me. Blue eyes laughing at me. Blue eyes laughing.

They might all be down there, for all I know. Huw and Moi and Em and Gran and Ceri and everybody. Ah, a wonderful thing it would be if I saw Mam coming up out of the Lake now and shouting: Come here you little monkey. Been up to mischief with that old Huw again.

I'll shout, just to see if there's an echo. Mam-a-a-m. Mam-a-a-m. Mam-a-a-m. Ah yes, indeed.

* * *

Is this the Voice, I wonder? Yes, this is it:

I am the Queen of the Black Lake, rejected by the Beautiful One.

My kingdom is the grievous waters that lie beyond the ultimate sorrow; whose bitterness did sweeten the waters of Marah.

I am learned in the chemistry of tears; I assembled them in the cauldron of the centuries, then dissected and reduced them to their elements.

Eternal and fleeting, sad and joyful, momentous and without significance was the task; as like the seed in the womb, I hurried from cell to cell, from person to person, in my quest.

To fight and to lose and to win and to be vanquished was my lot; to battle and to conquer and to squirm beneath the boot of the oppressor.

As we remember the garden, his crying out loud.

I knew the thrill of the morning and did revel therein until surfeiting; thereafter surfeiting beyond surfeit.

I raised my voice unto the firmament, even to the very joists of Heaven's floor; and like comets did my cries return unto my lips.

The showers of my repentance washed me purer than the laughter of a newborn babe; and rinsed me cleaner than the lowing of a lamb.

But then did I return unto the quest and take hold the baby's head, planting my red kiss upon his cheeks and turning his spittle into an issue of blood.

Pass me that pot under the bed. Wherefore may ravening beasts tear down the tender firstfruits?

I sent forth my hounds; and watched as they returned with the tyrant in their jaws.

My chariots rushed forth upon the wheels of the hurricane; and dragged my oppressors to their appointed stations.

I had them brought before me; and fairly did I divide my judgements among them.

And, with hands so dextrous did I skilfully complete the noose; and with luxurious tenderness did I prove the blade upon flesh.

Serves him right. But he was my brother, you know.

My innocence sought out the mysteries of the woodland; and deciphered with prophecy and music the melody of the birds.

I dreamed the dreams of the pig nuts; and watched them flourish in the wilderness.

I walked humbly upon the smooth pathway of the sanctified places; and saw the fruit of their vines anointing the elect.

I hungered for the bread of life and was satisfied; I thirsted for the living wine and was turned out into the sun, my thirst unquenched.

I swallowed the sun; and took the moon for a pillow to my resting place.

I plundered the stars' number; and with promiscuous eyes did lure the clouds into the depths of my kingdom.

I commanded her to come from the firmament and bow before me; she with eyes of bluest blue who did according to my word.

Therefore with Angels and Archangels and with the entire Company of Heaven.

GLOSSARY

Adwy Gap
Allt Hill
Allt Goch Red Hill
Bonc Rhiwia Quarrybank slopes
Braich Headland
Bron or Fron Hill
Bryn Hill
Bwlch Gap, pass
Cae Field
Cafn Trough
Ceunant Ravine, gorge
Clawdd Ditch
Cwt Crydd Cobbler's shed
Foel Bare hill
Ffridd Pasture
Ffwd stream
Garnedd Cairn
Garth Enclosure, garden, hill or
  ridge
Gorlan Sheepfold
Lôn Lane, road

Lôn Goed Wood Lane
Lôn Newydd New Lane
Llan Church
Nant Valley
Nant Ycha Upper valley
Pant Valley
Pen Top, end or head
Pen Pennog Herring head
Penwaig Herrings
Pen y Foel The top of Bald
  Hill
Rallt Ddu The Black Hill
Rallt Wen The White Hill
Rhiw Hill, ascent or slope
Tal End
Tal Cafn Trough End
Tan Under
Tan Bryn Beneath a hill
Tan Fron Beneath a hill
Terfyn Boundary
Waun Moor
Wen White